"We are," said Gale, "most ordinary, uncomplicated people from the year 2498, almost five centuries in your future. The span of time between you and us is about the same as the span of time between the American voyages of Columbus and your present day.

"We are traveling through time and I will not even attempt to try to explain how it is done. In fact, the best I could do would be to give you a very inadequate layman's explanation."

"You say," said the Secretary of State, "that you are transporting yourselves through time back to the present moment. May I ask how many of you intend to make the trip?"

"Under ideal circumstances, Mr. Williams, I would hope all of us."

"You mean your entire population? Your intention is to leave your world of 2498 empty of any human beings?"

"That, sir, is our desperate hope."

Clifford D. Simak
Our Children's Children

A BERKLEY MEDALLION BOOK
PUBLISHED BY
BERKLEY PUBLISHING CORPORATION

First appeared in IF

G. P. Putnam's Sons
200 Madison Avenue
New York, New York 10016

Library of Congress Catalog Card Number: 73-78644
SBN 425-02759-7

BERKLEY MEDALLION BOOKS are published by
Berkley Medallion Publishing Corporation
200 Madison Avenue
New York, N.Y. 10016

BERKLEY MEDALLION BOOKS ® TM 757.375

Printed in the United States of America

Berkley Medallion Edition, FEBRUARY, 1975

BENTLEY PRICE, photographer for Global News Service, had put a steak on the broiler and settled down in a lawn chair, with a can of beer in hand, to watch it, when the door opened underneath an ancient white oak tree and people started walking out of it.

It had been many years since Bentley Price had been astounded. He had come, through bitter experience, to expect the unusual and to think but little of it. He took pictures of the unusual, the bizarre, the violent, then turned around and left, sometimes most hurriedly, for there was competition such as the AP and the UPI, and an up-and-coming news photographer could allow no grass to grow beneath his feet, and while picture editors certainly were not individuals to be feared, it was often wise to keep them mollified.

But now Bentley was astounded, for what was happening was not something that could easily be imagined, or ever reconciled to any previous experience. He sat stiff in his chair, with the beer can rigid in his hand and with a glassy look about his eyes, watching the people walking from the door. Although now he saw it wasn't any door, but just a ragged hole of darkness which quivered at the edges and was somewhat larger than any ordinary door, for people were marching out of it four and five abreast.

They seemed quite ordinary people, although they were dressed a bit outlandishly, as if they might be coming home from a masquerade, although they weren't masked. If they all had been young, he would have thought they were from a university or a youth center or something of the sort, dressed up in the crazy kind of clothes that college students wore, but while some of them were young, there were a lot of them who weren't.

One of the first who had walked out of the door onto the lawn was a rather tall and thin man, but graceful in his thinness when he might have gangled. He had a great unruly mop of iron-gray hair and his neck looked like a turkey's. He wore a short gray skirt that ended just above his knobby knees and a red shawl draped across one shoulder and fastened at his waist by a belt that also held the skirt in place and he looked, Bentley told himself, like a Scot in kilts, but without the plaid.

Beside him walked a young woman dressed in a white and flowing robe that came down to her sandaled feet. The robe was belted and her intense black hair, worn in a ponytail, hung down to her waist. She had a pretty face, thought Bentley—the kind of prettiness that one very seldom saw, and her skin, what little could be seen of it, was as white and clear as the robe she wore.

The two walked toward Bentley and stopped in front of him.

"I presume," said the man, "that you are the proprietor."

There was something wrong with the way he talked. He slurred his words around, but was entirely understandable.

"I suppose," said Bentley, "you mean do I own the joint."

"Perhaps I do," the other said. "My speech may not be of this day, but you seem to hear me rightly."

"Sure I do," said Bentley, "but what about this day? You mean to tell me you speak different every day?"

"I do not mean that at all," said the man. "You must pardon our intrusion. It must appear unseemly. We'll endeavor not to harm your property."

"Well, I tell you, friend," said Bentley, "I don't own the place. I'm just holding down the homestead for an absent owner. Will you ask those people not to go tramping over flower beds? Joe's missus will be awful sore if she comes home and finds those flowers messed up. She sets store by them."

All the time that they'd been talking, people had been coming through the door and now they were all over the place and spilling over into the yards next door and the neighbors were coming out to see what was going on.

The girl smiled brightly at Bentley. "I think you can be easy about the flowers," she said. "These are good people, well-intentioned folks, and on their best behavior."

"They count upon your sufferance," said the man. "They are refugees."

Bentley took a good look at them. They didn't look like refugees. In his time, in many different parts of the world, he had photographed a lot of refugees. Refugees were grubby people and they usually packed a lot of plunder, but these people were neat and clean and they carried very little, a small piece of luggage, perhaps, or a sort of attaché case, like the one the man who was speaking with him had tucked underneath one arm.

"They don't look like refugees to me," he said. "Where are they refugeeing from?"

"From the future," said the man. "We beg utmost indulgence of you. What we are doing, I assure you, is a matter of life and death."

That shook Bentley up. He went to take a drink of beer and then decided not to and, reaching down, set the beer can on the lawn. He rose slowly from his chair.

"I tell you, mister," he said, "if this is some sort of publicity stunt I won't lift a camera. I wouldn't take no shot of no publicity stunt, no matter what it was."

"Publicity stunt?" asked the man, and there could be no doubt that he was plai ly puzzled. "I am sorry, sir. What you say eludes me."

Bentley took a close look at the door. People still were coming out of it, still four and five abreast, and there seemed no end to them. The door still hung there, as he first had seen it, a slightly ragged blob of darkness that quivered at the edges, blotting out a small section of the lawn, but behind and beyond it he could see the trees and shrubs and the play set in the back yard of the house next door.

If it was a publicity stunt, he decided, it was a top-notch job. A lot of PR jerks must have beat their brains out to dream up one like this. How had they rigged that ragged hole and where did all the people come from?

"We come," said the man, "from five hundred years into the future. We are fleeing from the end of the human race. We ask your help and understanding."

Bentley stared at him. "Mister," he asked, "you wouldn't kid me, would you? If I fell for this, I would lose my job."

"We expected, naturally," said the man, "to encounter disbelief. I realize there is no way we can prove our origin. We ask you, please, to accept us as what we say we are."

"I tell you what," said Bentley. "I will go with the gag. I will take some shots, but if I find it's publicity. . . ."

"You are speaking, I presume, of taking photographs."

"Of course I am," said Bentley. "The camera is my business."

"We didn't come to have photographs taken of us. If you have some compunctions about this matter, please feel free to follow them. We will not mind at all."

"So you don't want your pictures taken," Bentley said fiercely. "You're like a lot of other people. You get into a jam and then you scream because someone snaps a picture of you."

"We have no objections," said the man. "Take as many pictures as you wish."

"You don't mind?" Bentley asked, somewhat confused.

"Not at all."

Bentley swung about, heading for the back door. As he turned, his foot caught the can of beer and sent it flying, spraying beer out of the hole.

Three cameras lay on the kitchen table, where he had been working with them before he'd gone out to broil the steak. He grabbed up one of them and was turning back toward the door when he thought of Molly. Maybe he better let Molly know about this, he told himself. The guy had said all these people were coming from the future and if that were true, it would be nice for Molly to be in on it from the start. Not that he believed a word of it, of course, but it was mighty funny, no matter what was going on.

He picked up the kitchen phone and dialed. He grumbled at himself. He was wasting time when he should be taking pictures. Molly might not be home. It was Sunday and a nice day and there was no reason to expect to find her home.

Molly answered.

"Molly, this is Bentley. You know where I live?"

"You're over in Virginia. Mooching free rent off Joe while he is gone."

"It ain't like that at all. I'm taking care of the place for him. Edna, she has all these flowers. . . ."

"Ha!" said Molly.

"What I called about," said Bentley, "is would you come over here?"

"I will not," said Molly. "If you have in mind making passes at me, you have to take me out."

"I ain't making passes at no one," Bentley protested. "I got people walking out of a door all over the back yard. They say they're from the future, from five hundred years ahead."

"That's impossible," said Molly.

"That's what I think, too. But where are they coming from? There must be a thousand of them out there. Even if they're not from the future, it ought to be a story. You better haul your tail out here and talk with some of them. Have your byline in all the morning papers."

"Bentley, this is on the level?"

"On the level," Bentley said. "I ain't drunk and I'm not trying to trick you out here and. . . ."

"All right," she said. "I'll be right out. You better call the office. Manning had to take the Sunday trick himself this week and he's not too happy with it, so be careful how you greet him. But he'll want to get some other people out there. If this isn't just a joke. . . ."

"It's not any joke," said Bentley. "I ain't crazy enough to joke myself out of any job."

"I'll be seeing you," said Molly.

She hung up.

Bentley had started to dial the office number when the screen door slammed. He looked around and the tall, thin man stood just inside the kitchen.

"You'll pardon me," the tall man said, "but there seems to be a matter of some urgency. Some of the little folks need to use a bathroom. I wonder if you'd mind. . . ."

"Help yourself," said Bentley, making a thumb in the direction of the bath. "If you need it, there's another one upstairs."

Manning answered after a half a dozen rings.

"I got a story out here," Bentley told him.

"Out where?"

"Joe's place. Out where I am living."

"O.K. Let's have it."

"I ain't no reporter," said Bentley. "I ain't supposed to get you stories. All I do is take the pictures. This is a big story and I might make mistakes and I ain't paid to take the heat. . . ."

"All right," said Manning wearily. "I'll dig up someone to send out. But Sunday and overtime and all, it better be a good one."

"I got a thousand people out in the backyard, coming through a funny door. They say they're from the future. . . ."

"They say they're from the what!" howled Manning.

"From the future. From five hundred years ahead."

"Bentley, you are drunk. . . ."

"It don't make no never mind to me," said Bentley. "It's no skin off me. I told you. You do what you want."

He hung up and picked up a camera.

A steady stream of children, accompanied by some adults, were coming through the kitchen door.

"Lady," he said to one of the women, "there's another one upstairs. You better form two lines."

2

STEVE WILSON, White House press secretary, was heading for the door of his apartment and an afternoon with Judy Gray, his office secretary, when the phone rang. He retraced his steps to pick it up.

"This is Manning," said the voice at the other end.

"What can I do for you, Tom?"

"You got your radio turned on?"

"Hell, no. Why should I have a radio turned on?"

"There's something screwy going on," said Manning. "You should maybe know about it. Sounds like we're being invaded."

"Invaded!"

"Not that kind of invasion. People walking out of nothing. Say they're from the future."

"Look here—if this is a gag. . . ."

"I thought so, too," said Manning. "When Bentley first called in. . . ."

"You mean Bentley Price, your drunken photographer?"

"That's the one," said Manning, "but Bentley isn't drunk. Not this time. Too early in the day. Molly's out there now and I have sent out others. AP is on it now and. . . ."

"Where is this all going on?"

"One place is over across the river. Not far from Falls Church."

"One place, you say. . . ."

"There are others. We have it from Boston, Chicago, Minneapolis. AP just came in with a report from Denver."

"Thanks, Tom. I owe you."

He hung up, strode across the room and snapped on a radio.

". . . so far known," said the radio. "Only that people are marching out of what one observer called a hole in the landscape. Coming out five and six abreast. Like a marching army, one behind the other, a solid stream of them. This is happening in Virginia, just across the river. We have similar reports from Boston, the New York area, Minneapolis, Chicago, Denver, New Orleans, Los Angeles. As a rule, not in the cities themselves, but in the country just beyond the cities. And here is another one—Atlanta, this time."

There was a quiver in the deadpan voice, betraying momentary unprofessional excitement.

"No one knows who they are or where they come from or by what means they are coming. They are simply here, walking into this world of ours. Thousands of them and more coming every minute. An invasion, you might call it, but not a warlike invasion. They are coming emptyhanded. They are quiet and peaceable. They're not bothering anyone. One unconfirmed report is that they are from the future, but that, on the face of it, is impossible. . . ."

Wilson turned the radio to a whisper, went back to the phone and dialed.

The White House switchboard answered.

"That you, Della? This is Steve. Where is the President?"

"He's taking a nap."

"Could you get someone to wake him? Tell him to turn on the radio. I am coming in."

"But, Steve, what is going on? What is. . . ."

He broke the connection, dialed another number. After a time, Judy came on the line.

"Is there something wrong, Steve? I was just finishing packing the picnic basket. Don't tell me. . . ."

"No picnic today, sweetheart. We're going back to work."

"On Sunday!"

"Why not on Sunday? We have problems. I'll be right along. Be outside, waiting for me."

"Damn," she said. "There goes my plan. I had planned to

make you, right out in the open, on the grass, underneath the trees."

"I shall torture myself all day," said Wilson, "thinking what I missed."

"All right, Steve," she said. "I'll be outside waiting on the curb."

He turned up the radio. ". . . fleeing from the future. From something that happened in their future. Fleeing back to us, to this particular moment. There is, of course, no such thing as time travel, but there are all these people and they must have come from somewhere. . . ."

3

SAMUEL J. HENDERSON stood at the window, looking out across the rose garden, bright in the summer sun.

Why the hell, he wondered, did everything have to happen on Sunday, when everyone was scattered and it took no end of trouble to get hold of them? It had been on another Sunday that China had exploded and on still another that Chile had gone down the drain and here it was again—whatever this might be.

The intercom purred at him and, turning from the window, he went back to the desk and flipped up the key.

"The Secretary of Defense," said his secretary, "is on the line."

"Thank you, Kim," he said.

He picked up the phone. "Jim, this is Sam. You've heard?"

"Yes, Mr. President. Just a moment ago. On the radio. Just a snatch of it."

"That's all I have, too. But there seems no doubt. We have to do something, do it fast. Get the situation under control."

"I know. We'll have to take care of them. Housing. Food."

"Jim, the armed forces have to do the job. There is no one else who can move fast enough. We have to get them under shelter and keep them together. We can't let them scatter. We have to keep some sort of control over them, for a time at least. Until we know what is going on."

"We may have to call out the guard."

"I think," said the President, "perhaps we should. Use every resource at your command. You have inflatable shelters. How about transportation and food?"

"We can handle things for a few days. A week, maybe. Depends upon how many there are of them. In a very short time, we'll need help. Welfare. Agriculture. Whoever can lend a hand. We'll need a lot of manpower and supplies."

"You have to buy us some time," said the President. "Until we have a chance to look at what we have. You'll have to handle it on an emergency basis until we can settle on some plan. Don't worry too much about procedures. If you have to bend a few of them, we'll take care of that. I'll be talking to some of the others. Maybe we can all get together sometime late this afternoon or early evening. You are the first to call in. I've heard from none of the others."

"The CIA? The FBI?"

"I would imagine they both might be moving. I haven't heard from either. I suppose they'll be reporting in."

"Mr. President, do you have any idea. . . ."

"None at all. I'll let you know as soon as possible. Once you get things moving, get in touch again. I'll need you, Jim."

"I'll get on it immediately," said the Secretary.

"Fine, then. I'll be seeing you."

The intercom purred.

"Steve is here," said the President's secretary.

"Send him in."

Steve Wilson came through the door.

Henderson motioned toward a chair. "Sit down, Steve. What have we got?"

"It's spreading, sir. All over the United States and Europe. Up in Canada. A few places in South America. Russia. Singapore. Manila. Nothing yet from China or Africa. So far, no explanation. It's fantastic, sir. Unbelievable. One is tempted to say it can't be happening. But it is. Right in our laps."

The President removed his glasses, placed them on the desk top, pushed them back and forth with his fingertips.

"I've been talking with Sandburg. The army will have to get them under shelter, feed them, care for them. How's the weather?"

"I didn't look," Wilson said, "but if I remember correctly

from the morning broadcasts, good everywhere except the Pacific Northwest. It's raining there. It's always raining there."

"I tried to get State," said the President. "But, hell, you never can get State. Williams is out at Burning Tree. I left word. Someone's going out to get him. Why does everything always have to happen on Sunday? I suppose the press is gathering."

"The lounge is filling up. In another hour they'll be pounding at the door. I will have to let them in, but I can hold them for a while. By six o'clock, at the latest, they'll expect some sort of statement."

"Tell them we're trying to find out. The situation is under study. You can tell them the armed services are moving rapidly to help these people. Stress the help. Not detention—help. The guard may have to be called out to do the job. That is up to Jim."

"Maybe, sir, in another hour or two we'll know more of what is going on."

"Maybe. You have any thoughts on the matter, Steve?"
The press secretary shook his head.

"Well, we'll find out. I expect to be hearing from a lot of people. It seems incredible we can sit here, knowing nothing."

"You'll probably have to go on TV, sir. The people will expect it."

"I suppose so."

"I'll alert the networks."

"I suppose I had better talk with London and Moscow. Probably Peking and Paris. We're all in this together; we should act together. Williams, soon as he calls in, will know about that. I think I'd better phone Hugh, at the UN. See what he thinks."

"How much of this for the press, sir?"

"The TV, I guess. Better keep the rest quiet for the moment. You have any idea how many of these people are invading us?"

"UPI had an estimate. Twelve thousand an hour. That's in one place. There may be as many as a hundred places. The count's not in."

"For the love of God," said the President, "a million an hour. How will the world take care of them? We have too many people now. We haven't got the housing or the food. Why, do you suppose, are they coming here? If they are from the future, they would have historical data. They would know the problems they'd create."

"A compelling reason, said the secretary. "Some sort of desperation. Certainly they'd know we are limited in our capacity to put them up and keep them. It would have to be life or death for them to do it."

"Children of our children," said the President, "many times removed. If they're truly from the future, they are our descendants. We can't turn our backs on them."

"I hope everyone feels the same about it," said Wilson. "They'll create an economic pinch if they keep coming and in an economic pinch there will be resentment. We talk about the present generation gap. Think of how much greater that gap will be when not two generations, but a number are involved."

"The churches can help a lot," said the President, "if they will. If they don't, we could be in trouble. Let one loudmouthed evangelist start some pulpit thumping and we've had it."

Wilson grinned. "You're talking about Billings, sir. If you think it would be all right, I could get in touch with him. We knew one another back in college days. I can talk with him, but I don't know what good I'll do."

"Do what you can," said the President. "Reason with him. If he refuses to see reason, we'll find someone who can really lean on him. What really bothers me is the welfare population. Bread out of their mouths to feed all these extra mouths. It'll take fast footwork to keep them in line. The labor unions may be scared by all the extra manpower, but they are hardheaded people, all of them. A man can talk to them. They understand economics and you can make some sense to them."

The intercom came to life. The President thumbed the lever.

"Secretary Williams on the line, sir."

Wilson stood up to leave. The President reached for the phone. He looked up at Wilson.

"Stay close," said the President.

"I intend to, sir," said Wilson.

4

ALL the buttons on Judy's phone were blinking. She was talking quietly into the transmitter. The spindle on her desk was festooned with notes.

When Wilson came into the office, she hung up. The lights kept on with their blinking.

"The lounge is full," she said. "There is one urgent message. Tom Manning has something for you. Said it is top important. Shall I ring him?"

"You carry on," said Wilson. "I'll get him."

He sat down at his desk, hauled the phone close and dialed.

"Tom, this is Steve. Judy said it is important."

"I think it is," said Manning. "Molly has someone. Seems to be a sort of leader of the gang out in Virginia. Don't know how his credentials run, if there are credentials. But the thing is, he wants to talk with the President. Says he can explain. In fact, he insists on explaining."

"Has he talked with Molly?"

"Some. But not important stuff. He is reserving that."

"It has to be the President?"

"He says so. His name is Maynard Gale. He has a daughter with him. Name of Alice."

"Why don't you ask Molly to bring them along. Back way, not out in front. I'll notify the gate. I'll see what can be done."

"There's just one thing, Steve."

"Yes?"

"Molly found this guy. She has him hidden out. He is her exclusive."

"No," said Wilson.

"Yes," insisted Manning. "She sits in on it. It has to be that way. God damn it, Steve, it is only fair. You can't ask us to share this. Bentley snagged him first and Molly hung onto him."

"What you're asking me to do would ruin me. You know that as well as I do. The other press associations, the *Times*, the *Post*, all the rest of them. . . ."

"You could announce it," said Manning. "You'd get the information. All we want is an exclusive interview with Gale. You owe us that much, Steve."

"I'd be willing to announce that Global brought him in," said Wilson. "You'd be given full credit for it."

"But no exclusive interview."

"You have the man right now. Get your interview. Get it first, then bring him in. That would be your privilege. I might not like it, Tom, but there's not a thing I could do to stop it."

"But he won't talk until he's seen the President. You could release him to us once he's talked."

"We have no hold on him. Not at the moment, anyhow. We would have no right to release him to anyone. And how do you know he's what he says he is?"

"I can't be sure, of course," said Manning. "But he knows what is going on. He's part of what is going on. He has things all of us need to know. You wouldn't have to buy his story. You could listen, then exercise your judgment."

"Tom, I can't promise anything at all. You know I can't. I'm surprised you asked."

"Call me back after you've thought it over," Manning said.

"Now, wait a second, Tom."

"What is it now?"

"It seems to me you might be running on thin ice. You're withholding vital information."

"We have no information."

"A vital source of information, then. Public policy may be at issue. And what is more, you are holding the man against his will."

"We're not holding him. He's sticking tight to us. He figures we are the only ones who can get him to the White House.''

"Well, impeding him. Refusing to give him the assistance that he needs. And—I can't be sure of this, I can only guess—you might be dealing with the equivalent of an ambassador.''

"Steve, you can't lean on me. We've been friends too long. . . .''

"Let me tell you something, Tom. I'm not going along with this. Friendship or not. I have a hunch I could get a court order within the hour.''

"You couldn't get away with it.''

"You'd better talk to your lawyer. I'll look forward to hearing from you.''

He slammed down the phone and stood up.

"What was that all about?'' asked Judy.

"Tom tried to bluff me.''

"You were pretty rough on him.''

"Damn it, Judy, I had to be. If I had knuckled under—I couldn't knuckle under. In this job, you don't make any deals.''

"They're getting impatient out there, Steve.''

"OK. You better let them in.''

They came in with a rush, quietly, orderly, finding their accustomed seats. Judy closed the doors.

"You have anything for us, Steve?'' AP asked.

"No statement,'' said Wilson. "Really not anything at all. I guess all I have to say is that I'll let you know as soon as there is anything to tell. As of less than half an hour ago, the President knew no more about this than you do. He will have a statement later, as soon as he has some data to base a statement on. I guess the only thing I can tell you is that the armed forces will be assigned the job of getting these people under shelter and providing food and other necessities for them. This is only an emergency measure. A more comprehensive plan will be worked out later, perhaps involving a number of agencies.''

"Have you any idea,'' asked the Washington *Post,* "who our visitors are?''

"None at all,'' said Wilson. "Nothing definite. Not who they are, or where they come from, or why they came or how.''

"You don't buy their story they are coming from the future?''

16

"I didn't say that, John. We maintain the open mind of ignorance. We simply do not know."

"Mr. Wilson," said the New York *Times*, "has any contact been made with any of the visitors who can supply us facts? Have any conversations been initiated with these people?"

"At the moment, no."

"Can we assume from your answer that such a conversation may be imminent?"

"Actually, no such assumption would be justified. The administration is anxious, naturally, to learn what it's all about, but this event began happening not a great deal longer than an hour ago. There simply has been no time to get much done. I think all of you can understand that."

"But you do anticipate there'll be some conversations."

"I can only repeat that the administration is anxious to know what is going on. I would think that sometime soon we may be talking with some of the people. Not that I know of any actual plans to do so, but simply that it seems it would be an early logical course of action to talk with some of them. It occurs to me that members of the press may already have talked with some of them; you may be way ahead of us."

"We have tried," said UPI, "but none of them is saying much. It's almost as if they had been coached to say as little as possible. They will simply say they have come from the future of five hundred years ahead and they apologize for disturbing us, but explain it was a matter of life and death for them to come. Beyond that nothing. We are simply getting nowhere with them. I wonder, Steve, will the President be going on television?"

"I would think he might. I can't tell you when. I'll let you know immediately that a time is set."

"Mr. Wilson," asked the *Times*, "can you say whether the President will talk with Moscow or London or some of the other governments?"

"I'll know more about that after he talks with State."

"Has he talked with State?"

"By now, perhaps he may have. Give me another hour or so and I may have something for you. All I can do now is assure you I'll give you what I have as soon as the situation develops."

"Mr. Press Secretary," said the Chicago *Tribune*, "I suppose it has occurred to the administration that the addition to the world's population of some two and a half million an hour. . . ."

"You're ahead of me there," said Wilson. "My latest figure was something over a million an hour."

"There are now," said the *Tribune*, "about two hundred of the tunnels or openings or whatever you may call them. Even if there should be no more than that, it means that within less than forty-eight hours more than a billion people will have emerged upon the earth. My question is how is the world going to be able to feed that many additional people?"

"The administration," Wilson told the *Tribune*, "is very acutely aware of the problem. Does that answer your question?"

"Partially, sir. But how is it proposed to meet the problem?"

"That will be a matter for consultation," said Wilson, stiffly.

"You mean you won't answer it?"

"I mean that, at the moment, I can't answer it."

"There is another similar question," said the Los Angeles *Times*, "concerning the advanced science and technology that must exist in a world five hundred years ahead. Has there been any consideration given. . . ."

"There has not," said Wilson. "Not yet."

The New York *Times* arose. "Mr. Wilson," he said, "we seem now to be moving far afield. Perhaps later some similar questions will be possible to answer."

"I would hope so, sir," said Wilson.

He stood and watched the press corps file back into the lobby.

5

THE army was having trouble.

Lieutenant Andrew Shelby phoned Major Marcel Burns. "Sir, I can't keep these people together," he reported. "They are being kidnapped."

"What in hell are you talking about, Andy? Kidnapped?"

"Well, maybe not being kidnapped, actually. But people are taking them in. There is one big house full of them. There must be twenty or more of them inside of it. I talked with the owner. Look here, I told him, I have to keep these people together. I can't let them get scattered. I've got to load them up and take them where they have shelter and food. Lieutenant, said this man, you don't have to worry about the people I have here. If food and shelter is your only worry, you can stop your worrying. They are my house guests, sir, and they have food and shelter. And he was not the only one. That was only one house. Other houses, all up and down the street, they have them, too. The whole neighborhood has them. Everyone is taking them in. That's not the whole story, either. People are driving in from miles away to load them up and take them off to take care of them. They're being scattered all over the countryside and I can't do a thing about it."

"Are they still coming out of that door or whatever it is?"

"Yes, sir, they are still coming out of it. They have never stopped. It's like a big parade. They just keep marching out of it. I try to keep them together, sir, but they wander and they scatter and they are taken up by all the people in the neighborhood and I can't keep track of them."

"You've been transporting some of them?"

"Yes, sir. As fast as I can load them up."

"What kind of people are they?"

"Just ordinary people, sir. Far as I can see. No different from us, except that they got a sort of funny accent. They dress funny. Some of them in robes. Some of them in buckskins. Some of them in—oh, hell, they have all kinds of clothes. Like they were at a masquerade. But they are polite and cooperative. They don't give us no trouble. It's just that there are so many of them. More of them than I can haul away. They scatter, but that ain't their fault. It's the people who invite them home. They are friendly and real nice, but there are just too many of them."

The major sighed. "Well, carry on," he said. "Do the best you can."

6

THE buttons on Judy's telephone had never stopped their blinking. The lounge was jammed with waiting newsmen. Wilson got up from his desk and moved over to the row of clacking teletypes.

Global News was coming up with its fifth new lead.

WASHINGTON (GN)—Millions of visitors who say they are from 500 years in the future continued to come to the present world this afternoon, pouring in steady streams from more than 200 "time tunnels."

There has been general public reluctance to accept their explanation that they are from the future, but it is now beginning to gain some acceptance in official quarters, not so much in Washington as in some capitals abroad. Beyond the assertion that they are from the future, however, the refugees will add little else in the way of information. It is confidently expected that in the next few hours more information may be forthcoming. So far, in the confusion of the situation, no one who can be termed a leader or a spokesman has emerged from the hordes of people pouring from the tunnels. But there are some indications that such a spokesman may now have been located and that soon his story will be told. The distribution of the tunnels are worldwide and have been reported from every continent.

An unofficial estimate places the number of people

passing through them at close to two million an hour. At this rate . . .

"Steve," said Judy, "Tom Manning is on the phone."

Wilson went back to his desk.

"Have you got your court order yet?" Manning asked.

"Not yet. I gave you time."

"Well, you can get it any time you want to. Our attorney says you can."

"I don't think I'll need it."

"Matter of fact, you won't. Molly is already on her way. With Gale and his daughter. She'll be there in twenty minutes, more or less, depending on the traffic. It is getting hairy out there. Sightseers pouring in and a slew of army trucks."

"Tom," said Wilson, "there is something I want to say. I know why you had to do it. You simply had to try."

"Steve, there's one thing more."

"What is it, Tom?"

"Gale talked a little to Molly. Not much. There was one thing he asked her to pass along. Something that he said couldn't wait."

"You're passing it along?"

"He said to station an artillery piece in front of each of the time tunnels. High explosive rounds. If anything happens, fire straight into the tunnel. Don't pay any attention to the people who may be in it, but fire. If necessary, keep on firing."

"Any idea of what could happen?"

"He wouldn't say. Just that we would know. Said the explosion would knock out the tunnel, collapse it, put an end to it. You'll take it from here?"

"I'll take it from here."

"I'm not going to use it now," said Manning. "Not right away."

Wilson hung up, picked up the Presidential phone.

"Kim," he asked, "when can I get in?"

"He's on the phone now. There are other calls holding. There are people with him. How important is this, Steve?"

"Top important. I have to see the man."

"Come on in. I'll slip you in as soon as possible."

"Judy," said Wilson. "Molly Kimball is coming in the back

22

way. She'll have two of the refugees with her.''

"I'll call the gate," said Judy. "And security. When they get here?''

"If I'm not back, send them in to Kim.''

7

SANDBURG, Secretary of Defense, and Williams, Secretary of State, sat on a davenport in front of the President's desk. Reilly Douglas, Attorney General, was in a chair at its corner. They nodded to Wilson when he came into the room.

"Steve," said the President, "I know that what you have must be important." It was just short of a rebuke.

"I think so, Mr. President," said Wilson. "Molly Kimball is bringing in one of the refugees who says he is a spokesman for at least the Virginia group. I thought you might want to see him, sir."

"Sit down, Steve," said the President. "What do you know about this man? Is he really a spokesman? An accredited spokesman?"

: "I don't know," said Wilson. "I would suppose he might have some credentials."

"In any case," said the Secretary of State, "we should listen to what he has to say. God knows, no one else has been able to tell us anything."

Wilson took a chair next to the Attorney General and settled into it.

"The man sent a message ahead," he said. "He thought we should know as soon as possible. He suggested an artillery piece, firing high explosive rounds, be placed in front of every door or time tunnel or whatever the people are coming out of."

"There is some danger, then?" asked the Secretary of Defense.

Wilson shook his head. "I don't know. He apparently was not specific. Only if anything happened at any tunnel we should fire an explosive charge directly into it. Even if there were people in it. To disregard the people and fire. He said it would collapse the tunnel."

"What could happen?" asked Sandburg.

"Tom Manning passed on the word from Molly. Quoted the spokesman as saying we would know. I got the impression it was precautionary only. He'll be here in a few minutes. He could tell us."

"What do you think?" the President asked the others. "Should we see this man?"

"I think we have to," said Williams. "It's not a matter of protocol, because in the situation as it stands we have no idea what protocol might be. Even if he isn't what he says he is, he can give us information, and so far we have none at all. It isn't as if we were accepting him as an ambassador or official representative of those people out there. We could use our judgment as to how much of his story we'd accept."

Sandburg nodded gravely. "I think we should have him in."

"I don't like the idea of a press association bringing him in," said the Attorney General. "They'd not be particularly disinterested parties. There would be a tendency to palm their own man off on us."

"I know Tom Manning," said Wilson. "Molly, too, for that matter. They won't trade on it. Maybe they would have if he had talked to Molly, but he wouldn't talk to anyone. The President, he said, was the only man he'd talk with."

"The act of a public-spirited citizen," said the Attorney General.

"If you're talking about Manning and Molly," said Wilson, "yes, I think so. Your opinion may differ from mine."

"After all," said the Secretary of State, "we'd not be seeing him in any official capacity unless we made it so. We'd not be bound by anything we say."

"And," said the Secretary of Defense, "I want to hear more about blowing up those tunnels. I don't mind telling you they have bothered me. I suppose it is all right so long as only people are coming out of them. But what would we do if something else started coming through?"

25

"Like what?" asked Douglas.

"I don't know," said Sandburg.

"How deeply, Reilly, does your objection go?" the President asked the Attorney General.

"Not deeply," said Douglas. "Just a lawyer's reaction against irregularity."

"Then I think," said the President, "that we should see him." He looked at Wilson. "Do you know, has he got a name?"

"Maynard Gale," said Wilson. "He has his daughter with him. Her name is Alice."

The President nodded. "You men have the time to sit in on this?"

They nodded.

"Steve," said the President. "You as well. He's your baby."

8

THE village had known hunger, but now the hunger ended. For, sometime in the night, a miracle had happened. High up in the sky, just beyond the village, a hole had opened up and out of the hole poured a steady stream of wheat. The foolish boy with the crippled leg, who belonged to no one, who had simply wandered into the village, who was crippled in his mind as well as in his body, had been the first to see it. Skulking through the night, skulking as well as he could with one leg that dragged, unable to sleep, looking for the slightest husk that he could steal and chew upon, he had seen the grain plunging from the sky in the bright moonlight. He had been frightened and had turned about to run, but his twisting hunger would not let him run. He had not known what it was to start with, but it was something new and it might be something he could eat and he could not run away. So, frightened still, he had crept upon it and finally, seeing what it was, had rushed upon it and thrown himself upon the pile that had accumulated. He had stuffed his mouth, chewing and gasping, gulping to swallow the half-chewed grain, strangling and coughing, but stuffing his mouth again as soon as he managed to clear his throat. The overloaded stomach, unaccustomed to such quantities of food, revolted, and he rolled down off the pile and lay upon the ground, weakly vomiting.

It was there that others found him later and kicked him out of the way, for with this wondrous thing that had happened and that had been spotted by a man of the village who had happened to go out to relieve himself, they had no time for a foolish, crippled boy who had merely attached himself to the village and did not belong there.

The village was aroused immediately and everyone came with baskets and with jars to carry off the wheat, but there was far more than enough to fill all the receptacles that the village had, so the headmen got together and made plans. Holes were dug in which the grain was dumped, which was no way to treat good wheat, but it must be hidden, if possible, from the sight of others and it was the only thing they could think of to do immediately. With the dryness and the drought upon the land there was no moisture in the ground to spoil the wheat and it could be safely buried until the time when something else could be devised to store it.

But the grain kept pouring from the sky and the ground was baked and hard to dig and they could not dispose of the pile, which kept growing faster than they could dispose of it.

And in the morning soldiers came and, thrusting the villagers to one side, began hauling the wheat away in trucks.

The miracle kept on happening, the wheat pouring from the sky, but now it was a less precious miracle, not for the village alone, but for a lot of other people.

9

"I would suppose," said Maynard Gale, "that you would like to know exactly who we are and where we're from."

"That," agreed the President, "might be an excellent place to start."

"We are," said Gale, "most ordinary, uncomplicated people from the year 2498, almost five centuries in your future. The span of time between you and us is about the same as the span of time between the American voyages of Christopher Columbus and your present day.

"We are traveling here through what I understand you are calling, in a speculative way, time tunnels, and that name is good enough. We are transporting ourselves through time and I will not even attempt to try to explain how it is done. Actually I couldn't even if I wanted to. I do not understand the principles, other than in a very general way. If, in fact, I understand them at all. The best that I could do would be to give you a very inadequate layman's explanation."

"You say," said the Secretary of State, "that you are transporting yourselves through time back to the present moment. May I ask how many of you intend to make the trip?"

"Under ideal circumstances, Mr. Williams, I would hope all of us."

"You mean your entire population? Your intention is to leave your world of 2498 empty of any human beings?"

"That, sir, is our heartfelt hope."

"And how many of you are there?"

"Give or take a few thousand, two billion of us. Our population, as you will note, is somewhat less than yours at the present moment and later I will explain why this. . . ."

"But why?" asked the Attorney General. "Why did you do this? You must know that the world's economy cannot support both your population and our own. Here in the United States, perhaps in a few of the more favored countries of the world, the situation can be coped with for a limited period of time. We can, as a matter of utmost urgency, shelter you and feed you, although it will strain even our resources. But there are other areas of the Earth that could not do this, even for a week."

"We are well aware of that," said Maynard Gale. "We are trying to make certain provisions to alleviate the situation. In India, in China, in some African and South American areas we are sending back in time not only people, but wheat and other food supplies, in the hope that whatever we can send through may help. We know how inadequate these provisions will be. And we know as well the stress which we place upon all the people of this time. You must believe me when I say we did not arrive at our decision lightly."

"I would hope not," said the President, somewhat tartly.

"I think," said Gale, "that in your time you may have taken note of published speculations about whether or not there are other intelligences in the universe, with the almost unanimous conclusion that there must surely be. Which raises the subsidiary question of why, if this is so, none of these intelligences has sought us out, why we've not been visited. The answer to this, of course, is that space is vast and the distances between stars are great and that our solar system lies far out in one of the galactic arms, far from the greater star density in the galactic core, where intelligence might have risen first. And then there is the speculation concerning what kind of people, if you want to call them that, might come visiting if they should happen to do so. Here I think the overwhelming, although by no means unanimous, body of opinion is that by the time a race had developed star-roving capability they would have arrived at a point of social and ethical development where they would pose no threat.

"And while this may be true enough, there would always be

exceptions and we, it seems, up in our own time, have become the victims of one of these exceptions."

"What you are saying," said Sandburg, "is that you have been visited, with what appear to have been unhappy results. Is that why you sent ahead the warning about the planting of artillery?"

"You haven't done that yet? From the tone of your voice. . . ."

"There has not been the time."

"Sir, I plead with you. We discussed the possibility that some of them might break through the defenses we set up and invade the tunnels. We have strong defenses, of course, and there are strict orders, which will be carried out by devoted men, to destroy any tunnel where this might happen, but there always is the chance that something could go wrong."

"But your warning was so indefinite. How will we know if something. . . ."

"You would know," said Gale. "There would be no doubt at all. Take a cross between a grizzly bear and a tiger, elephant size. Let it move so fast that it seems no more than a blur. Give it teeth and claws and a long, heavy tail armed with poison spines. Not that they look like bears or tigers, or even elephants. . . ."

"You mean they carry nothing but claws and teeth. . . ."

"You're thinking of weapons, sir. They don't need weapons. The are unbelievably fast and strong. They are filled with thoughtless bloodlust. They take a lot of killing. Tear them apart and they still keep coming on. They can tunnel under fortifications and tear strong walls apart. . . ."

"It is unbelievable," said the Attorney General.

"You are right," said Gale, "but I am telling you the truth. We have held them off for almost twenty years, but we can foresee the end. We foresaw it a few years after they first landed. We knew we only had one chance—to retreat, and the only place we could retreat to was into the past. We can hold them off no longer. Gentlemen, believe me, five hundred years from now the human earth is coming to an end."

"They can't follow you through time, however," said the President.

"If you mean, can they duplicate our time capability, I am fairly sure they can't. They're not that kind of being."

"There is a serious flaw in your story," said the Secretary of State. "You describe these alien invaders as little more than ferocious beasts. Intelligent, perhaps, but still mere animals. For intelligence to be transformed into a technology such as would be necessary to build what I suppose you would call a spaceship, they would require manipulatory members—hands, tentacles, something of the sort."

"They have them."

"But you said. . . ."

"I'm sorry," said Gale. "It cannot all be told at once. They have members armed with claws. They have other members that end in the equivalent of hands. And they have manipulatory tentacles as well. Theirs is a strange evolutionary case. In their evolutionary development, apparently, and for what reason we do not know, they did not trade one thing for another, as had been the case in the evolution of the creatures of the Earth. They developed new organs and abilities, but they let loose of none of those they already had. They hung onto everything. They loaded the evolutionary deck in favor of themselves.

"I would suspect that if they wished they could build most efficient weapons. We have often wondered why they didn't. Our psychologists think they know why it is. They postulate that these aliens are a warrior race. They glory in killing. They may have developed their space-traveling capability for no other reason than that they might find other things to kill. Killing is a personal thing for them, an intensely personal experience, like religion once was for the human race. And since it is so personal, it must be done personally, with no mechanical aids. It must be done with claws and fangs and poison tail. They may feel about mechanical killing aids as an accomplished swordsman of some hundreds of years ago must have regarded the first guns, with contempt as a cowardly way to fight. Perhaps each one of them must continually reassert his manhood or his beasthood, his selfhood, perhaps, and the only means by which he can do this is slaughter, personally accomplished. Their individual standing, their regard for themselves, the regard of their fellows for them, may be based upon the quality and the quantity of their killing. Once a fight is done they eat their victims, or as many of them as they can, but whether this is for sustenance or is a ritualistic matter, of course we do not know. In fact, we

32

know little of them. There has been, as you can imagine, no communication with them. We have photographed them and we have studied them dead, but this is only superficial to any understanding of them. They do not fight campaigns. They seem to have no real plan of battle, no strategy. If they had, they would have wiped us out long ago. They make sudden raids and then they retire. They make no attempt to hold territory as such. They don't loot. All they seem to want is killing. At times it has seemed to us that they have deliberately not wiped us out, as if they were conserving us, making us last as long as possible so we'd still be there to satisfy their bloodlust.''

Wilson glanced at the girl sitting on the sofa beside Gale and caught on her face a shadow of terror.

"Twenty years, you say," said Sandburg. "You held these things off for twenty years."

"We are doing better now," said Gale. "Or at least we were doing better before we left. We have weapons now. At first we had none. The Earth had been without war and weapons for a hundred years or more when their spaceship came. They would have exterminated us then if they had fought a total war, but as I have explained, it has not been total war. That gave us time to develop some defense. We fabricated weapons, some of them rather sophisticated weapons, but even your weapons of today would not be enough—your nuclear weapons, perhaps, but no sane society. . . .''

He stopped in some embarrassment, waited for a moment and then went on. "We killed a lot of them, of course, but it seemed to make no difference. There always seemed as many of them as ever, if not more. Only the one spaceship came, so far as we could determine. It could not have carried many of them, large as it was. The only answer to their numbers seems to be that they are prolific breeders and that they reach maturity in an incredibly short time. They don't seem to mind dying. They never run or hide. I suppose, again, that it is their warrior's code. Nothing quite so glorious as a death in battle. And they took so damn much killing. Kill a hundred of them and let one get through and it more than evens the score. I imagine that we lived the same kind of fear-ridden life as the old American pioneers who lived in the shadow of Indian raids. If we had stayed, they would eventually have wiped us out. Even trying to conserve us, as they may have been trying, they still would have exterminated us. That is why we're here.

"It is impossible, I think, for the human race to accept the sort of creatures they are. There is nothing that we know that can compare with them. The traditionally blood-crazed weasel in the chicken coop is a pale imitation of them."

"Perhaps," said the President, "in view of what we have been told, we should do something now in regard to that artillery."

"We have, of course," the Attorney General pointed out, "no real evidence. . . ."

"I would rather," said Sandburg sharply, "move without ironclad evidence than find it suddenly sitting in my lap."

The President reached for his phone. He said to the Secretary of Defense, "You can use this phone. Kim will put through the call."

"After Jim has made his call," said State, "perhaps I should use the phone. We'll want to get off an advisory to the other governments."

MISS EMMA GARSIDE turned off the radio and sat in silence, bolt upright in her chair, in something approaching awe of herself for the brilliance of the idea that had just occurred to her. It was not often (well, actually never before) that she had felt that way, for although a proud woman, she also was inclined to be mousy in both her actions and her thought. The pride she had was a secret pride, divulged only occasionally and in a very guarded manner to Miss Clarabelle Smythe, her very closest friend. It was a pride she held close within herself, for comfort, although there were times she flinched a little when she remembered the undoubted horse thief and the man who had been hanged for a rather heinous offense. She had never mentioned either the horse thief or the hanged man to her good friend Clarabelle.

The Sunday sun of afternoon slanted through the westward-facing windows, falling on the worn carpeting where the aged cat slept, tightly rolled into a ball. In the garden at the rear of the dowdy house on the dowdy street the catbird was calling sassily—perhaps preparing for a new inroad on the raspberry patch—but she paid it no attention.

It had cost a deal of money, she thought, and a lot of work and letter writing and some traveling, but it had been worth it, she told herself, all the money and the time. For there was no one else in this little town who could trace back their blood as far as she—to the Revolution and beyond, back to English days and little English villages that lay sunken deep in time. And while there had been a horse thief and a hanged man and others of somewhat dubious character and undistinguished lineage, they had been offset by country squires and sturdy yeomen, with even the hint of an ancient castle somewhere in the background, although she never had quite honestly been able to authenticate the castle.

And now, she thought, and now! She had carried her family research back as far as human ingenuity and records went. Now could she—would she dare—proceed in the opposite direction—forward into the future? She knew all the old ancestors and here, she told herself, was the opportunity to acquaint herself with all the new descendants. If these people were really what the radio hinted they might be, it surely could be done. But if it were to be done, she would have to do it, for there would be no records. She would have to go among them—those who came from the area of New England—and she would have to ask her questions and she might ask many different people before she got a clue. Are there, my dear, any Garsides or Lamberts or Lawrences in your family tree? Well, then, if you think so, but don't really know, is there anyone who would? Oh, yes, my dear, of course it is most important—I cannot begin to tell you how important.

She sat in the chair unstirring, while the cat slept on and the catbird screamed, feeling in her that strange sense of family that had driven her all these years, and which, given this new development, might drive her further yet.

11

"SO," said the President, leaning back in his chair, "as we have it so far, the Earth some five hundred years from now is being attacked by beings from out of space. It is impossible for the people of that day to cope with them and their only recourse is to retreat back into the past. Is that a fairly accurate summary of what you've told us?"

Gale nodded. "Yes, sir, I would say it is."

"But now that you are here—or a lot of you are here and more coming all the time—what happens now? Or have you had no opportunity to plan ahead?"

"We have plans," said Gale, "but we will need some help."

"What I want to know," said the Attorney General, "is why you came back to us. Why to this particular moment in time?"

"Because," said Gale, "you have the technology that we need and the resources. We made a very thorough historical survey and this particular time slot, give or take ten years, seemed to suit our purpose best."

"What kind of technology are you thinking of?"

"A technology that is capable of fabricating other time machines. We have the plans and the specifications and the labor force. We will need materials and your forbearance. . . ."

"But why more time machines?"

"We do not intend to stay here," said Gale. "It would be unfair to do so. It would put too great a strain on your economy. As it is, we are putting a great strain upon it. But we could not

37

stay up there in the future. I hope you understand that we had to leave.''

''Where will you be going?'' asked the President.

''Back deep into time,'' said Gale. ''To the mid-Miocene.''

''The Miocene?''

''A geological epoch. It began, roughly, some twenty-five million years ago, lasted for some twelve million years.''

''But why the Miocene? Why twenty-five million years? Why not ten million, or fifty million or a hundred million?''

''There are a number of considerations,'' said Gale. ''We have tried to work it out as carefully as we can. For one thing, the main reason, I would guess, grass first appeared in the Miocene. Paleontologists believe that grass appeared at the beginning of the Miocene. They base their belief upon the development of high-crowned cheek teeth in the herbivores of that time. Grass carries abrasive minerals and wears down the teeth. The development of high-crowned teeth that grew throughout the animal's lifetime would be an answer to this. The teeth are the kind that one would expect to find in creatures that lived on grass. There is evidence, too, that during the Miocene more arid conditions came about which led to the replacement of forests by extensive grass prairies that supported huge herds of grazing animals. This, say the paleontologists, began with the dawn of the Miocene, twenty-five million years ago, but we have chosen as our first target twenty million years ago, just in case the paleontologists' timetable may be in error, although we do not believe it is.''

''If that is where you're heading,'' asked the Attorney General, ''why are you stopping here? Your time tunnels, I assume, the ones you used to reach us, would have carried you that far.''

''That is true, sir. But we didn't have the time. This move had to be made as rapidly as possible.''

''What has time to do with it?''

''We can't go into the Miocene without implements and tools, with no seed stocks or agricultural animals. We have all those up in our own time, of course, but it would have taken weeks to gather and transport them to the tunnel mouths. There was also the matter of capacity. Every tool or bag of seed or head of livestock would mean it would take longer to move the people. Given the time and without the pressure of the aliens we would have done it that way, going directly to the Miocene. But the logistics were impossible. The monsters knew there was something going on and as soon as they found out what it was, we knew they would attack the tunnel heads. We felt we had to move as swiftly as we could, to save as many people as we could. So we arrive here emptyhanded."

"You expect us to furnish you with all the things you need?"

"Reilly," the President said quietly, "it seems to me you are being somewhat uncharitable. This is not a situation that we asked for nor one that we expected, but it is one we have and we must deal with it as gracefully and as sensibly as we can. As a nation we have helped and still are helping other less-favored peoples. It is a matter of foreign policy, of course, but it is as well an old American tendency to hold out a helping hand. These people coming out of the tunnels located on our soil are, I would imagine, native Americans, our own kind of people, our own descendants, and it doesn't seem to me we should balk at doing for them what we have done for others."

"If," the Attorney General pointed out, "any of this is true."

"That is something," the President agreed, "we must determine. I imagine that Mr. Gale would not expect us to accept what he has told us without further investigation when that is possible. There is one thing, Mr. Gale, that rather worries me. You say that you plan on going back to a time when grass has evolved. Do you intend going blind? What would happen if, when you got there, you find the paleontologists were mistaken about the grass, or that there are other circumstances that would make it very difficult for you to settle there?"

"We came here blind, of course," said Gale. "But that was different. We had fairly good historic evidence. We knew what we would find. You can't be as certain when you deal with time spans covering millions of years. But we think we have an answer fairly well worked out. Our physicists and other scientists have developed, at least theoretically, a means of communication through a time tunnel. We hope to be able to send through an advance party that can explore the situation and then report back to us.

"One thing I have not explained is that, as we have it developed now, our time travel capability is in one direction only. We can go into the past; we cannot move futureward. So, if any advance party is sent back and finds the situation untenable, they have no recourse other than to stay there. Our great fear is that we may have to keep readjusting the destination of the tunnels and may have to send out, and abandon, several advance parties. We hope not, of course, but it is a possibility, and if necessary it will be done. Our people, gentlemen, are quite prepared to face such a situation. We have men up in your future guarding the tunnel heads who do not expect to travel through the tunnels. They are well aware that there will come a time when each tunnel must be destroyed and that they and whoever else may not have made it through the tunnels must then face death.

"I don't tell you this to enlist your sympathy. I only say it to assure you that whatever dangers there may be we are quite willing, ourselves, to face. We shall not call upon you for more than you are willing to give. We shall be grateful, of course, for anything that you may do."

"Kindly as I may feel toward you," said the Secretary of State, "and much as I am disposed, short of a certain natural skepticism, to believe what you have told us, I am considerably puzzled by some of the implications. What is happening now, right here this minute, will become a matter of historical record. It stands to reason that it now becomes a part of history that you read up in the future. So you knew before you started how it all came out. You would have had to know."

"No," said Gale, "we did not know. It was not in our history. It hadn't, strange as it may sound, happened yet. . . ."

"But it had," said Sandburg. "It must have."

"Now," said Gale, "you are getting into an area that I do not understand at all, philosophical and physical concepts, strangely intertwined and, so far as I am concerned, impossible of any real understanding. It is something that our scientific community gave a lot of thought to. At first we asked ourselves if it lay within our right to change history, to go back into the past and introduce factors that would change the course of events. We wondered what effects such history changing would have and what would happen to the history that we already have. But now we are told that it will have no effect at all upon the history that already has been laid down. I know all this must sound impossible to you and I admit that I don't fully understand all the factors myself. The human race passed this way once before, when our ancestors were moving futureward and this thing that is happening now did not happen then. So the human race moved up to our future and the alien invaders came. Now we come back to escape the aliens and this event now is happening, history has been changed and from this moment forward nothing will be quite the same. History has been changed, but not our history, not the history that led forward to the moment that we left. Your history has been changed. By our action you are on another time track. Whether on this second time track the aliens will attack, we cannot be sure, but the indications are they will. . . ."

"This," said Douglas flatly, "is a lot of nonsense."

"Believe me," said Gale, "it is not willing nonsense. The men who worked it out, who thought it through, are honorable and accomplished scholars."

"This is nothing," said the President, "that we can resolve at the moment. Since it is done, we can safely put it off until another day. After all, what's done is done and we have to live with it. There is one thing else that puzzles me."

"Please say it, sir," said Gale.

"Why go back twenty million years? Why so far?"

"We want to go back far enough so that our occupation of that segment of Earth's time cannot possibly have any impact on the rise of mankind. We probably will not be there too long. Our historians tell us that man, in his present state of technology, cannot look forward to more than a million years on Earth, perhaps much less than that. In a million years, in far less than a million years, we'll all be gone from Earth. We are right now, I mean we were up in our own time, if we had been left undisturbed, only a few centuries from true spaceship capability. Given a few thousand years we will have developed deep space capability and probably will be gone from Earth. Once man can leave the Earth, he probably will leave it. Give him a million years and he surely will be gone."

"But you will have impact back there," Williams pointed out. "You'll use up natural resources. You'll use coal and iron, you'll tap oil and gas. You will. . . ."

"Some iron. Not enough that it will be noticed. With so little left up there five hundred years from now, we've learned to be very frugal. And no fossil fuel at all."

"You'll need energy."

"We have fusion power," said Gale. "Our economy would be a great shock to you. We now make things to last. Not ten years, or twenty, but for centuries. Obsolescence no longer is a factor in our economy. As a result, our manufacturing up in 2498, is less than one percent of what yours is today."

"That's impossible," said Sandburg.

"By your present standards, perhaps," admitted Gale. "Not by ours. We had to change our life-style. We simply had no choice. Centuries of overuse of natural resources left us impoverished. We had to do with what we had. We had to find ways in which to do it."

"If what you say about man remaining on the Earth for no longer than another million years is true," said the President; "I don't quite understand why you have to travel back the twenty million. You could go back only five and it would be quite all right."

Gale shook his head. "We'd be getting too close, then, to the forerunners of mankind. True, man as we can recognize him, rose no more than two million years ago, but the first primates came into being some seventy million years ago. We'll be intruding on those first primates, of course, but perhaps with no great impact, and it would be impossible for us to miss them, for to go beyond them would place us in the era of the dinosaurs, which would not be a comfortable time period. Not just the dinosaurs alone, but a number of other things. The critical period for mankind, the appearance of the forerunners of the australopithecines, could not have been later than fifteen million years ago. We can't be certain of these figures. Most of our anthropologists believe that if we went back only ten million it probably would be safe enough. But we want to be sure. And there is no reason why we can't go deeper into time. So the twenty million. And there is another thing, as well. We want to leave room enough for you."

Douglas leaped to his feet. "For us!" he yelled.

The President raised a restraining hand. "Wait a minute, Reilly. Let's have the rest of it."

"It makes good sense," said Gale, "or we think it does. Consider this—just five hundred years ahead lies the invasion from outer space. Yes, I know, because of the second time track we have thrown you on, it may not happen, but our scholars think it will, they're almost sure it will. So why should you move forward to meet it? Why not go back with us? You've got a five-hundred-year margin. You could make use of it. You could go back, not in a hurry as we'll be going, but over the course of a number of years. Why not leave Earth empty and go back to make a new beginning? It would be a fresh start for the human race. New lands to develop. . . .''

"This is sheer insanity!" shouted Douglas. "If we, your ancestors, left, you'd not be up there to start with and. . . .''

"You're forgetting what he explained to us," said Williams, "about a different time track."

Douglas sat down. "I wash my hands of it," he said. "I'll have no more to do with it."

"We couldn't go back with you," said Sandburg. "There are too many of us and. . . .''

"Not with us. Like us. Together there would be far too many of us. There are too many of you now. Here is the chance, if you will take it, to reduce your population to more acceptable numbers. We go back twenty million years. Half of you go back nineteen million years, the other half eighteen million years. Each group of us would be separated by a million years. We'd not interfere with one another."

"There is one drawback," said Williams. "We'd not be like you. We would have a disastrous impact on mankind. We'd use up the coal, the iron. . . .''

"Not," said Gale, "if you had our philosophy, our viewpoint, our technologies. . . .''

"You would give these things to us? The fusion power . . .''

"If you were going back," said Gale, "we'd insist on it."

The President rose. "I think," he said, "we have reached a point where we must stop. There are many things that must be done. We thank you, Mr. Gale, for coming to us and bringing along your lovely daughter. I wonder if we might have the privilege, later, of talking further with you."

"Certainly," said Gale. "It would be a pleasure. There are others of us that you should be talking with, men and women who know far more than I do about many aspects of the situation you should be informed on."

"Would it be agreeable to the two of you," asked the President, "to be my house guests? I'd be glad to put you up."

Alice Gale spoke for the first time. She clapped her hands together, delighted. "You mean here in the White House?"

The President smiled. "Yes, my dear, in the White House. We'd be very glad to have you."

"You must pardon her," her father said. "It happens that the White House is a special interest of hers. She has studied it. She has read everything about it she can lay her hands on. Its history and its architecture, everything about it."

"Which," said the President, "is a great compliment to us."

12

THE people still were marching from the door, but now there were military policemen to direct them either right or left, to keep the mouth of the tunnel free for those who came pressing on behind, moving in tight ranks, and others to hold back the crowds of curious sightseers who had flocked into the area. A bullhorn voice bawled out directions and when the bullhorn fell silent, the tiny chatter of a radio could be heard, a radio left on in one of the hundreds of cars parked up and down the street, some of them against the curb, others—in a fine display of the disrespect of property—pulled up onto lawns. Military trucks and personnel carriers trundled down the street, halted long enough to take on a load of refugees, then went roaring off. But the people came out of the tunnel faster than the trucks could cart them off and the great mass of people kept pushing outward, covering ever-widening blocks.

Lieutenant Andrew Shelby spoke into the phone to Major Marcel Burns on the other end: "We ain't more than making a dent in them, sir. Christ, I never saw so many people. It would be easier if we could get some of the sightseers out of the area, and we're doing what we can, but it's hard to get them untangled and they don't want to leave and we haven't got the manpower to do a job of it. We've closed off all civilian traffic to the area and the radio has been asking people not to come out here, but they still are coming or are trying to come and the roads are clogged. I hate to think of what it will be like once it gets dark.

How about them engineers who were supposed to come out here and put up some flood lights?''

"They're on their way," said Burns. "Hang in there, Andy, and do everything you can. We got to get those people out of there.''

"I need more carriers," the lieutenant said.

"I'm feeding them in," the major told him, "as fast as I can lay my hands on them. And another thing—there'll be a gun crew coming out.''

"We don't need no gun. What we need a gun for?''

"I don't know," the major said. "All I know it is on its way. No one told me what it was coming for.''

13

"YOU can't honestly believe this story," Douglas protested. "It's too preposterous to admit of any credence. It is something jerked out of the middle of a science fiction story. I tell you we've been had."

Williams said quietly, "So are all these people coming out of the time tunnels preposterous. There has to be some explanation of them. Gale's may be a bit fantastic, but it holds together in a sort of zany fashion. I admit I have some difficulty. . . ."

"And his credentials," the Attorney General pointed out. "Identification rather than credentials. Ombudsman for the Washington community, a social service worker of some kind. No connection with any governmental unit. . . ."

"Maybe," said Williams, "they have no real government. You must realize, five centuries from now there would be changes."

"Steve," said the President, "what do you make of it? You are the man who brought him in."

"A waste of time," said Douglas.

"If you want me to vouch for his story," said Wilson, "I can't do that, of course."

"What did Molly say?" asked Sandburg.

"Nothing really. She simply turned him over to me. He told her none of the things that he told us, of that I'm sure, but she wormed out of him and his daughter some sort of story about what kind of world they came from. She said she was satisfied."

"Did Global News try to make a deal?" asked Douglas.

"Of course they did. Any news agency or any reporter worth his salt certainly would have tried. They'd have been delinquent in their job if they hadn't tried. But Manning didn't press too hard. He knew as well as I did. . . ."

"You didn't make a deal?" asked Douglas.

"You know he didn't," said the President.

"What I need right now," said Wilson, "is some indication of how much I should tell the press."

"Nothing," said Douglas. "Absolutely nothing."

"They know I've been in here. They know something is going on. They won't be satisfied with nothing."

"They don't need to know."

"But they do need to know," said Wilson. "You can't treat the press as an adversary. They have a definite function to perform. The people have a right to know. The press has played ball with us before and they will this time, but we can't ignore them. We have to give them something and it had better be the truth."

"I would think," said Williams, "that we should tell them we have information which tends to make us believe these people may be, as they say, from the future, but that we need some time to check. At the moment, we can make no positive announcement. We still are working on it."

"They'll want to know," said Sandburg, "why they are coming back. Steve has to have some sort of answer. We can't send him out there naked. And, besides that, they will know, within a short time, that we are placing guns in front of the tunnels."

"It would scare hell out of everyone," said Williams, "if it was known why the guns were being placed. There would be a worldwide clamor for us to use the guns to shut down the tunnels."

"Why don't we just say," suggested the President, "that the people of the future are facing some great catastrophe and are fleeing for their lives. The guns? I suppose we'll have to say something about them. We can't be caught in a downright falsehood. You can say they are no more than routine precaution."

"But only if the question should be raised," said Sandburg.

"OK," said Wilson, "but that isn't all of it. There'll be other questions. Have we consulted with other nations? How about the UN? Will there be a formal statement later?"

"You could say, perhaps," said Williams, "that we have contacted other governments. We have—that advisory about the guns."

"Steve," said the President, "you'll have to try to hold them off. We've got to get our feet under us. Tell them you'll be back to them later."

14

By Molly Kimball

WASHINGTON (Global News)—The people who are coming from the tunnels are refugees from time.

This was confirmed late today by Maynard Gale, one of the refugees. He refused to say, however, why they were fleeing from a future which he says lies 500 years ahead of us. The circumstances of their flight, he insisted, could only be revealed to a constituted government. He said he was making efforts to get in contact with an appropriate authority. He explained that he held the position of ombudsman for the Washington community in his future time and had been delegated to communicate with the federal government upon his arrival here.

He did, however, give a startling picture of the kind of society in which he lives, or rather, did live—a world in which there are no longer any nations and from which the concept of war has disappeared.

It is a simple society, he said, forced to become simple by the ecological problems that we face today. It is no longer an industrial society. Its manufacturing amounts to no more, perhaps less, than one percent of today's figure. What it does manufacture is made to last. The philosophy of obsolescense was abandoned only a short distance into our future, he said, in the face of dwindling natural resources, a dwindling about which economists and ecologists have been warning us for years.

Because its coal and fossil fuels are almost gone, the future world, said Gale, relies entirely for its energy on fusion power. The development of that type of power, he said, is the only thing that holds the delicate economic fabric of his world together.

The world of 500 years from now is highly computerized, with the greater part of the population living in "high rise" cities. Half a dozen towers, some of them reaching as high as a mile, will constitute a city. Urban sprawl is gone, leaving vast surface areas free for agricultural purposes. The cities are built, in large part, from converted scrap metal which in our day would have been buried in landfills, and are computer-operated, almost entirely automatic.

There is, Gale said, none of the great spread of wealth that is found in our world. No one is rich and there is none of the abject poverty that today oppresses millions. Apparently there has been not only a change in life style, but a change as well in life values. Life is simpler and kinder and less competitive; there are few eager beavers in that world of 500 years ahead. . . .

15

A crowd was gathering in Lafayette Park, quiet and orderly, as crowds had gathered through the years, to stand staring at the White House, not demanding anything, not expecting anything, simply gathering there in a dumb show of participation in a nation's crisis. Above the crowd, Andy Jackson still sat his rearing charger, with the patina of many years upon both horse and rider, friends to perching pigeons.

No one quite knew what this crisis meant or if it might even be a crisis. They had, as yet, no idea how it had come about or what it might mean to them, although there were a few among them who had done some rather specific, although distorted, thinking on the subject and were willing (at times, perhaps, insistent) on sharing with their neighbors what they had been thinking.

In the White House a flood of calls had started to come in and were stacking up—calls from members of the Congress, from party stalwarts ready with suggestions and advice, from businessmen and industrialists suddenly grown nervous, from crackpots who held immediate solutions.

A television camera crew drove up in their van and set up for business, taking footage of the Lafayette crowd and of the White House, gleaming in the summer sun, with a newsman doing a stand-up commentary against the background.

Straggling tourists trailed up and down the avenue, somewhat astonished at thus being caught up in the midst of history, and the White House squirrels came scampering down to the fence and through it out onto the sidewalk, sitting up daintily, with forepaws folded on their chests, begging for handouts.

16

ALICE GALE stood in the window, gazing across Pennsylvania Avenue to the gathering crowd in the park beyond it. She hugged herself in shivering ecstasy, not daring to believe that she actually was there, that she could be back in twentieth-century Washington, where history had been made, where legendary men had lived, and at this moment in the very room where crowned heads had slept.

Crowned heads, she thought. What an awful, almost medieval phrase. And yet it had a certain ring to it, a certain elegance that her world had never known.

She had caught a glimpse of the Washington Monument as she and her father had been driven into the White House grounds, and out there, just beyond it, a marble Lincoln sat in his marble chair, with his arms resting on its arms and his massive, whiskered face bearing that look of greatness, of sorrow and compassion that had quieted thousands into reverent silence as they came climbing up the stairs to stand face to face with him.

Just across the hallway her father was in the Lincoln bedroom, with its massive Victorian bed and the velvet-covered slipper chairs. Although, she recalled, Lincoln had never really slept there.

It was history back to life, she thought, history resurrected. And it was a precious thing. It would be something to remember always, no matter what might be ahead. It would be something to remember back in the Miocene. And what, she wondered with a little shiver, might the Miocene be like? If they ever got there, if the people of this time should decide to help them in getting there?

But whatever might happen, she had something she could say—"Once I slept in the Queen's Bedroom."

She turned from the window and looked in wonder once-again-renewed at the huge four-poster bed with its hangings and counterpane of rose and white, at the mahogany bookcase-secretary that stood between the windows, the soft white carpeting.

It was selfish of her, she knew, to be feeling this when so many others of her world at this very moment stood homeless and bewildered, unsure of their welcome, perhaps wondering if they would be fed and where they might lay their heads this night, but even as she tried, she could not rebuke herself.

17

"TERRY," said the President, speaking into the phone, "this is Sam Henderson."

"How good of you to call, Mr. President," said Terrance Roberts, on the other end. "What can I do for you?"

The President chuckled. "You maybe could do a lot for me. I don't know if you would. You've heard what's happening?"

"Strange things," said the labor leader. "A lot of speculation. Are you folks in Washington making any sense of it?"

"Some," said the President. "It would seem the people are really from the future. They're facing catastrophe up there and the only way they could escape was to run back into time. We haven't got the full story yet. . . ."

"But, Mr. President, time travel?"

"I know. It doesn't sound possible. I haven't talked to any of our physicists, although I intend to do so, and I suspect they'll tell me it's impossible. But one of the people who came through a time tunnel swears to us it is. If there was any other way to explain it, I'd be more skeptical than I am. But I'm forced by circumstances to accept the idea, at least provisionally."

"You mean all of them from up ahead are coming back? How many of them are there?"

"A couple of billion or so, I guess."

"But, Mr. President, how will we take care of them?"

"Well, that's really, Terry, what I wanted to talk with you

about. It seems they don't intend to stay here. They mean to go farther back in time—some twenty million years farther back in time. But they need help to do it. They need new time tunnels built and they'll need equipment to take back with them. . . ."

"We can't build time tunnels."

"They can show us how."

"It would cost a lot. Both in manpower and materials. Can they pay for it?"

"I don't know. I never thought to ask. I don't suppose they can. But it seems to me we have to do it. We can't let them stay on here. We have too many people as it is."

"Somehow, Mr. President," said Terrance Roberts, "I can sense what you want to ask me."

The President laughed. "Not only you, Terry. The industrialists as well—everyone, in fact, but I have to know beforehand what kind of cooperation I can expect. I wonder if you'd mind coming down here so a few of us can talk about it."

"Certainly, I could come down. Just let me know when you want me. Although I'm not just sure how much I can do for you. Let me ask around some, talk to some of the other boys. Exactly what do you have in mind?"

"I'm not entirely sure. That's something I'll need some help in working out. On the face of it, we can't do the kind of job that's called for under existing circumstances. The government can't assume alone the kind of costs that would be involved—I'm not thinking just of the tunnels. I have no idea so far what they would involve. But we would need to furnish the resources for an entire new civilization to start over once again and that would cost a lot of money. The taxpaying public would never stand for it. So we'll have to turn elsewhere for some help. Labor will have to help us, industry will have to help. We're facing a national emergency and it calls for some extraordinary measures. I don't even know how long we can feed all these people and. . . ."

"It's not only us," said Roberts. "It's the rest of the world as well."

"That's right. And they'll have to take some action, too. If there were time, we could put together some sort of international setup, but a thing like that takes time and we haven't got the time. To start with, at least, it has to be a national action."

"Have you talked to any of the other nations?"

"Britain and Russia," said the President. "Some of the others later. But not about this. Once we get an idea or two shaped up, we can see what some of the others think. Pool our ideas, trade them back and forth. But we can't take much time. Whatever we do we'll have to get started on almost immediately and work as fast as we can."

"You are sure there are people from up ahead who can explain these tunnels? Well enough so that our scientists and engineers can understand the principles involved and the technology well enough so it can be done—hell, Mr. President, this is sheer insanity. American labor building time tunnels! This must be all a dream. Or a bad joke."

"I'm afraid," said the President, "it is neither. We're in a mess, Terry. I don't know how bad a mess. I imagine it will be a day or two before we have the full story and know what we really face. All I ask right now is that you think about it. Get a few ideas together. Figure out what you can do. I'll let you know about coming down. No use coming now. We have to get a few things sorted out before we can talk. I'll be in touch as soon as I know a little more about it."

"Any time, Mr. President," said Roberts. "You let me know and I'll be there."

The President hung up and buzzed Kim. "Ask Steve to come in," he said when she opened the door. He tilted back in his chair and locked his hands behind his head, staring at the ceiling. Less than five hours ago, he thought, he'd stretched out for a nap, looking forward to a lazy Sunday afternoon. He didn't get many lazy afternoons and when they came he treasured them. He'd no more than shut his eyes than the world had fallen in on him. Christ, he asked himself, what am I to do? What can I do? What's the wise thing to do? Without half trying, a man could make a mistake or a number of mistakes and he sensed that in a situation such as this, he could not afford mistakes.

Steve Wilson came in the door. The President took his hands from behind his head and tilted forward in the chair.

"Have you had the press in, Steve?"

"No, sir, I haven't. They're pounding on the door, but I haven't let them in. I didn't have the guts to face them with the little that you gave me. I had been hoping. . . ."

"All right, then," said the President. "Your hope paid off.

57

You can give them all of it with two exceptions. You can't tell them why we have the guns planted. That still has to be simply normal precautions. And there must be no hint of Gale suggesting we go back in time with them.''

"I can't tell them, then, about why they're leaving the future. Nothing about the aliens?''

The President shook his head. "Simply say that this point has not been sufficiently clarified and needs more study before anything can be said of it.''

"They won't like it,'' said Wilson, "but I guess that I can manage. How about the TV? I have alerted the networks you may want time this evening.''

"How about ten o'clock? That's a little late, I suppose, but. . . .''

"It would be all right.''

"Then you set it up. Tell them only ten or fifteen minutes or so.''

"I'll draft up something for you to look at.''

"You have your hands full, Steve. I'll ask Brad and Frank to put it together.''

"They'll want to know if you've talked with anyone.''

"I talked with Sterling in London and Menkov in Moscow. You can tell them Menkov has talked with the Russian equivalent of our Gale and has substantially the same story we got. London still hadn't been contacted by anyone when I spoke with Sterling. You can say I plan to talk with other national leaders before the day is out.''

"How about a cabinet meeting? The question is sure to come up.''

"I've been seeing Cabinet members off and on during the last few hours. This is the first time since it's started there has been no one in this office. And I'll be conferring with people on the Hill, of course. Anything else you can think of, Steve?''

"There'll probably be a lot of other questions. I'll manage to field them. You can't anticipate them all. This will satisfy them.''

"Steve, what did you think of Gale? Your own personal opinion. How do you size him up?''

"It's hard to know,'' said Wilson. "No real impression, I'd think. Except that I can't figure out where he'd gain anything by not telling the truth, or at least the truth as he saw it. However you look at it, those people out there are in serious trouble and they look to us to help them. Maybe they have a thing or two to hide, maybe it's not exactly as Gale told it, but I think mostly it is. Hard as it may be to accept, I'm inclined to believe him."

"I hope you're right," said the President. "If we're wrong, they could make us awful fools."

18

THE chauffeured car went up the curving drive to the gracious mansion set well back from the street amid the flowers and trees. When it stopped before the portico, the chauffeur got out and opened the rear door. The old man fumbled out of it, groping with his cane. He petulantly struck aside the chauffeur's hand when he put it out to help.

"I still can manage to get out of a car alone," he panted, finally disengaging himself from it and standing, albeit a little shakily and unsure of himself, upon the driveway. "You wait right here for me," he said. "It may take a little while, but you wait right here for me."

"Certainly, Senator," said the driver. "Those stairs, sir —they look a little steep."

"You stay right here," said Senator Andrew Oakes. "You go sit behind the wheel. Time comes when I can't climb stairs, I'll go back home and let some young man have my seat. But not right yet," he said, wheezing a little, "not right now. Maybe in another year or two. Maybe not. Depends on how I feel."

He stumped toward the stairs, clomping his cane with weighty precision upon the driveway. He mounted the first step and stood there for a moment before attempting the next one. As he mounted each step, he looked to either side of him, glaring into the landscape, as if daring someone to remark upon his progress. Which was quite unnecessary, since there was no one there—except the driver, who had gone back to sit behind the wheel, studiously not watching the old man's progress up the stairs.

The door came open when he was crossing the pillared portico.

"I am glad to see you, Senator," said Grant Wellington, "but there was no need to make the trip. I could have come to your apartment."

The Senator stopped, planting himself sturdily before his host. "Nice day for a drive," he said, "and you said you would be alone."

Wellington nodded. "Family in New England and the servants' day off. We'll be quite alone."

"Good," said the Senator. "My place you never can be sure. People in and out. Phones ringing all the time. This is better."

He stumped into the entry. "To your right," said Wellington, closing the door.

The old man went into the study, shuffled across the carpeting, dropped into a huge, upholstered chair to one side of the fireplace. He laid his cane carefully on the floor beside him, looked around at the book-lined shelves, the huge executive-type desk, the comfortable furniture, the paintings on the wall.

"You have got it good, Grant," he said. "I sometimes worry about that. Maybe you have it too good."

"Meaning I won't fight. Will be afraid to dirty my hands."

"Something like that, Grant. But I tell myself I'm wrong. Did plenty of fighting in your day. Out in the business world." He gestured at the paintings. "Always suspicious of a man who owns a Renoir."

"How about a drink, Senator?"

"Late enough in the afternoon," said the Senator judiciously, "for a splash of bourbon. Great drink, bourbon. American. Has character. I remember you drink scotch."

"With you," said Wellington, "I drink bourbon."

"You been listening to what is happening?"

"Saw some of it on TV."

"Man could stub his toe," said the Senator, "on a thing like that. He could stub his toe real bad."

"You mean Henderson."

"I mean everybody. Easy thing to do."

Wellington brought the Senator his drink, went back to the

61

bar to pour his own. The Senator settled more deeply into the chair, fondling the glass. He took a drink, puffed out his cheeks in appreciation. "For a scotch man," he said, "you carry a good brand."

"I took my cue from you," said Wellington, coming back and sitting on a sofa.

"I imagine the man at 1600," said the Senator, "has a lot on his mind. Maybe more than he can handle. Terrible batch of decisions to be made. Yes, sir, a lot of them."

"I don't envy him," said Wellington.

"Most terrible thing that can happen to a man," said the Senator. "With election coming up next year. He'll have that on his mind and it won't help him any. Trouble is he has to say something, has to do something. Nobody else has to, but he has to."

"If you are trying to say that I should say nothing or do nothing, you are succeeding very well," said Wellington. "Never try to be subtle, Senator. You're not very good at it."

"Well, I don't know," said the Senator. "You can't come straight out and tell a man to keep his mouth shut."

"If these people are really from the future. . . ."

"Oh, they're from the future, all right. Where else could they come from?"

"Then you can't go wrong on them," said Wellington. "They are our descendants. What they are doing is like a bunch of kids running home after they got hurt."

"Well, now, I don't know," said the Senator, "although that's not exactly what I meant. It's not the people; it is old Sam up there in the White House. He's the one who's got to do something about it and he's bound to make mistakes and we got to watch careful to evaluate those mistakes of his. We can jump on some of them and some of them we can't. There may be even a few things he does that we have to go along with; we can't be too unreasonable. But the thing right now is not to commit ourselves. You know and I know there are a lot of people want that nomination next summer to run against old Sam, and I mean, if I can imagine it, that you are the one who gets it. Some of the other boys will think they see some opportunities in what the man up there does and they'll get anxious and start shooting off their mouths and I tell you, Grant, that the people won't remember who was first, but the one who happens to be right.''

"Of course, I appreciate your concern," said Wellington, "but it happens that you made this trip for nothing. I had no intention whatever of taking a position. I'm not sure right now there is a position one can take.''

The Senator held out his empty glass. "If you don't mind," he said, "another little splash."

Wellington poured another little splash, and the Senator settled back again.

"That matter of a position," he said, "is something that is going to require some long and prayerful thought. It has not become apparent yet, but there will be positions practically begging to be taken and a man must look them over good and select them very carefully. What you say about these folks being our descendants is all well and good. You being a man whose family history is long and proud would think that way, of course. But you got to remember that there are a lot of people with little family history and not proud of what they have, and these people, who make up the greatest part of the good old U.S.A., are not going to give a damn about them being their descendants. Maybe them being our descendants will make it all the worse. There are a lot of families these days that are having lots of trouble with their own immediate descendants.

"There are several millions of these people already through the tunnels and they still are pouring through and while we can hold up our hands in pious horror and ask how we are going to take care of them, the real gut reaction will come when those extra millions begin to have an effect on the economy. Food may suddenly get scarce and other things as well and prices will go up and there'll be a housing problem and a labor problem and there won't be goods enough to go around and while all this now is just economic talk, in a little while it will cease to be just economic talk and every man and woman in this fair land of ours will feel the impact of it and that's when there's hell to pay. And that's the time when a man like you must pick out his position and study all the angles before he settles on it."

"Good God," said Wellington, "this thing is happening out there—our own people of the future fleeing back to us—and here we sit, the two of us, and trying to figure out a good, safe political position. . . .''

"Politics," said the Senator, "is a very complicated and a most practical business. You've got to be hardheaded about it. You can't ever afford to get emotional about it. That's the first thing that you must remember—don't ever get emotional about anything at all. Oh, it's all right to appear to be emotional. Sometimes that has a certain appeal for the electorate. But before you can afford to get emotional you must have everything all figured out ahead of time. You may be emotional for effect, but never because you feel that way."

"It's not too attractive the way you put it, Senator. It leaves one with a slightly dirty taste."

"Sure, I know," said the Senator. "I know about that dirty taste myself. You just shut your mind to it, is all. It's all right, of course, to be a great statesman and a humanitarian, but before you get to be a statesman you have to be a dirty politician. You have to get elected first. And you never get elected without feeling just a little dirty."

He placed the glass on the table beside his chair, fumbled for his cane and found it, heaved himself erect.

"Now, you mind," he said, "before you go saying anything, you just check with me. I been through all this before, many times before. I guess you could say I have developed a political instinct for the jugular and I am seldom wrong. Up there on the Hill we hear things. There are some real good pipelines. I'll know when there's anything about to happen, so we'll have time to study it."

19

THE press conference had gone well. Arrangements had been made for the President's TV appearance. The clock on the wall ticked over to 6 P.M. The teletypes went on clacking softly to themselves.

Wilson said to Judy, "You'd better call it a day. It's time to close up shop."

"How about yourself?"

"I'll hang on for a while. Take my car. I'll call a cab and pick it up at your place."

He reached into his pocket, pulled out the keys and tossed them to her.

"When you get there," Judy said, "come up for a drink. I'll be up and waiting."

"It may be late."

"If it's too late, why bother going home? You left your toothbrush last time."

"Pajamas," he said.

"When did you ever need pajamas?"

He grinned at her lazily. "OK," he said. "Toothbrush, no pajamas."

"Maybe," said Judy, "it'll make up for this afternoon."

"What this afternoon?"

"I told you, remember. What I planned to do."

"Oh, that."

"Yes, oh, that. I've never done it that way."

"You're a shameless child. Now, run along."

"The kitchen will be sending coffee and sandwiches to the

press lounge. Ask them nice and they'll throw a crust to you.''

He sat and watched her go. She walked surely, but with a daintiness that always intrigued and puzzled him, as if she were a sprite who was consciously trying to make an earth creature of herself.

He shuffled the loose papers on the desk into a pile and stacked them to one side.

He sat quietly once that was done and listened to the strange mutterings of the place. Somewhere, far off, a phone rang. There was the distant sound of someone walking. Out in the lounge someone was typing and against the wall the wire machines went on with their clacking.

It was all insane, he told himself. The entire business was stark, staring crazy. No one in their right mind would believe a word of it. Time tunnels and aliens out of space were the sort of junk the high school crowd watched on television. Could it all, he wondered, be a matter of delusion, of mass hysteria? When the sun rose tomorrow, would it all be gone and the world back on the old familiar footing?

He shoved back the chair and got up. Judy's deserted console had a couple of lights flashing and he let them flicker. He went into the corridor and down it to the outer door. Out in the garden the heat of the summer day was cooling off, and long shadows thrown by the trees stretched across the lawn. The flower beds lay in all their glory—roses, heliotrope, geraniums, nicotiana, columbines and daisies. He stood, looking across the park to where the Washington Monument reared its classic whiteness.

Behind him he heard a footstep and swung around. A woman stood just a little distance off, dressed in a white robe that came down to her sandaled feet.

''Miss Gale,'' he said, a little startled. ''What a pleasant surprise.''

''I hope,'' she said, ''I have done nothing wrong. No one stopped me. Is it all right to be here?''

''Certainly. As a guest. . . .''

''I had to see the garden. I had read so much of it.''

''You have never been here, then?''

She hesitated. ''Yes, I have. But it was not the same. It was nothing like this.''

''Well,'' he said, ''I suppose that things do change.''

"Yes," she said, "they do."

"Is there something wrong?"

"No, I guess not." She hesitated again. "I see you don't understand. I can't imagine there is any reason why I shouldn't tell you."

"Tell me what? Something about this place?"

"It's this," she said. "Up in my time, up five hundred years ahead, there isn't any garden. There isn't any White House."

He stared at her.

"See," she said, "you don't believe it. You won't believe me. We have no nations there—we just have one big nation, although that's not exactly right. There aren't any nations and there isn't any White House. A few ragged, broken walls is all, a piece of rusted fence sticking from the ground that you stub your toe upon. There isn't any park and there aren't any flower beds. Now can you understand? Can you know what all this means to me?"

"But how? When?"

"Not right away," she said. "Not for a century or more. And now it may never happen. You're on a different time track now."

She stood there, a thin slip of a girl, in her chaste white robe, belted at the waist, talking of different time tracks and of a future when there would be no White House. He shook his head, bewildered. "How much do you understand?" he asked. "Of this time track business? I know your father mentioned it, but there was so much else. . . ."

"There are equations that you have to know to understand it all," she said. "There are, I suppose, only a few men who really understand it. But basically it's quite simple. It's a cause-and-effect situation and once you change the cause or, more likely, many causes, as we must have done in coming here. . . ."

He made a motion of futility with his hand. "I still can't believe it," he said. "Not just the time track, but all the rest of it. I woke up this morning and I was going on a picnic. You know what a picnic is?"

"No," she said, "I don't know what a picnic is. So we are even now."

"Someday I'll take you on a picnic."

"I wish you would," she said, "Is it something nice?"

67

20

BENTLEY PRICE came home a bit befuddled, but somewhat triumphant, for he had talked his way past a roadblock set up by the military, had yelled a jeep off the road, and honked his way through two blocks clotted by refugees and spectators who had stayed in the area despite all efforts by the MPs to move them out. The driveway was half-blocked by a car, but he made his way around it, clipping a rose bush in the process.

Night had fallen and it had been a busy day and all that Bentley wanted was to get into the house and collapse upon a bed, but before he did he must clear the car of cameras and other equipment, for it would never do, with so many strangers in the neighborhood, to leave it locked in the car, as had been his habit. A locked car would be no deterrent to someone really bent on thievery. He hung three cameras by their straps around his neck and was hauling a heavy accessories bag out of the car when he saw, with outrage, what had happened to Edna's flower bed.

A gun stood in the center of it, its wheels sunk deep into the soil, and around it stood the gun crew. The gun site was brightly lighted by a large spotlight that had been hung high in the branches of a tree and there could be no doubt of the havoc that had been wrought upon the flowers.

Bentley charged purposefully upon the gun, brushing aside one astounded cannoneer, to square off, like an embattled bantam rooster, before a young man who had bars upon his shoulder straps.

"You have your nerve," said Bentley. "Coming here when the owner happens to be gone. . . ."

"Are you the owner, sir?" asked the captain of the gun crew.

"No," said Bentley, "I am not, but I am responsible. I was left here to look out for the joint and. . . ."

"We are sorry, sir," said the officer, "if we have displeased you, but we had our orders, sir."

Bentley shrilled at him. "You had orders to set up this contraption in the middle of Edna's flower bed? I suppose the orders said to set up in the middle of a flower bed, not a few feet forward or a few feet back, but in the middle of a bed which a devoted woman has slaved to bring up to perfection. . . ."

"No, not precisely that," said the officer. "We were ordered to cover the mouth of the time tunnel and to do that we needed a clear line of fire."

"That don't make no sense," said Bentley. "Why would you want to cover the tunnel, with all them poor people coming out of it?"

"I don't know," said the officer. "No one bothered to explain to me. I simply got my orders and I'm about to carry them out, flower bed or no flower bed, owner or no owner."

"Somehow," said Bentley, "you don't sound like no gentleman to me and that's what you're supposed to be, ain't it, an officer and a gentleman. There wouldn't be any gentleman set up no gun in the middle of a flower bed and there wouldn't be any officer aim his gun at a bunch of refugees and. . . ."

A shrill scream split the night and Bentley spun around and saw that there was something very terrible happening in the tunnel. There were people still coming out of it, but they weren't marching out four and five abreast, the way they had before. They were running out of it, fighting to get out, and overriding them and plowing through them was a horror that Bentley, in that moment, never quite got sorted in his mind. He had the impression of wicked teeth and drooling jaws, of mighty talons protruding from massive, furry paws, of terrible power and ferocity, and quite by habit his hands went down to grip a camera and bring it to his eye.

Through the lens, he saw that there was not one, but two of the creatures, one almost through the tunnel and the other close behind. He saw the bodies of people flying through the air like limp dolls thrown about by children, and others that were crushed beneath the monster's treading feet. And he saw, as well, writhing tentacles, as if the creatures could not quite make up their minds if they were animals or octopi.

Behind him sharp orders rang out and almost at his elbow the gun belched sudden flame that lit up all the houses and the yards and gardens. A thunderclap concussion knocked him to one side and as he hit the ground and rolled, he saw a number of things slantwise out of the corner of his eyes. The tunnel had suddenly blinked out in an explosion that was little more than a continuation of the concussion, although it was more mind-numbing and nerve-shaking than the concussion and there were dead people and a dead monster that smoked as if it had been fried. But while one of the monsters lay upon the lawn beneath the great oak tree that had marked the tunnel, the other monster was very much alive and somehow the one live monster and the gun and gun crew were very much mixed up and people were running, screaming and in terror.

Bentley scrambled to his feet and took one quick glance around and in that single glance he saw the gun crew dead, ripped and flung and trampled, with the gun tipped over, smoke still trailing from its muzzle. From down the street came shrill, high screams and he caught, for an instant only, the flickering motion of something large and dark, moving very swiftly, whipping across one corner of a yard, with a picket fence exploding in a shower of white slivers as the dark thing went straight through it.

He sprinted around the corner of the house and burst through the kitchen door, clawing for the phone, dialing almost by instinct, praying that the line was open.

"Global News," said a raspy voice. "Manning."

"Tom, this is Bentley."

"Yes, Bentley. What is it now? Where are you?"

"I am home. Out at Joe's place. And I got some news."

"Are you sober?"

"Well, I stopped by a place I know and had a drink or two. Sunday, you know. None of the regular places open. And when I come home I found a gun crew out in the yard, right in Edna's flower bed. . . ."

"Hell," said Manning, "that is not any news. We had that a

70

couple of hours ago. They set up guns at all the tunnels for some reason."

"I know the reason."

"Well, now, that's nice," said Manning.

"Yeah, there was a monster come through the tunnel and. . . ."

"A monster! What kind of monster?"

"Well, I don't know," said Bentley. "I never got a real good look at it. And there wasn't only one monster. There was two of them. One of them the gun killed, but the other got away. It killed the gun crew and tipped over the gun and all the people ran screaming and it got away. I saw it bust right through a picket fence. . . ."

"Now, Bentley," said Manning, "stop talking quite so fast. Take it a little slow and tell me. You say one monster got away. There is a monster loose. . . ."

"There sure is. He killed the gun crew and maybe other people, too. The tunnel is shut down and there's a dead monster out there."

"Now tell me about the monster. What kind of monster was it?"

"I can't tell you that," said Bentley, "but I got pictures of it."

"Of the dead one, I suppose."

"No, the live one," said Bentley, his voice bright with scorn. "I wouldn't never bother with no dead monster when there's a live one."

"Now, listen, Bentley. Listen closely. Are you in shape to drive?"

"Sure, I'm in shape to drive. I drove out here, didn't I?"

"All right. I'll send someone else out there. And you—I want you to get in here as quickly as you can with the pictures that you have. And, Bentley. . . ."

"Yes?"

"You're sure you're right? There really was a monster?"

"I'm sure I'm right," said Bentley piously. "I only had a drink or two."

21

STEVE WILSON went into the press lounge in search of coffee and sandwiches. A dozen or so newsmen still were there.

"Anything new, Steve?" asked Carl Anders, of the AP.

Wilson shook his head. "Everything seems to be quiet. If there were anything of consequence going on; I think that I would know it."

"And tell us?"

"And tell you," Wilson said sharply. "You know damn well we've played fair with you."

"Yeah? How about the guns?"

"Simply routine emergency precaution. How about some sandwiches or did you guys eat them all?"

"Over there in the corner, Steve," said John Gates, of the Washington *Post*.

Wilson piled two sandwiches on a plate and got a cup of coffee. As he came back across the room, Gates slid over on the davenport where he had been lounging and patted a place beside him. Wilson sat down, putting the plate and cup of coffee on the table that stood in front of the davenport.

Anders came over to take a nearby chair. Henry Hunt, the New York *Times* man, sat down on the davenport on the other side of Wilson.

"It'. ᵅen a long day, Steve," he said.

Wilsc ʲit into a sandwich. "Rough," he said.

"What's going on right now?" asked Anders.

"Perhaps quite a bit. Nothing that I know of. There's nothing I can tell, nothing that I know."

Gates chuckled. "You can talk, can't you?"

"Sure I can talk. But I can't give you anything. You guys know procedure. If I should happen to say something that makes sense, it is off the record."

"Well, hell, yes, of course," said Anders. "You newspapered yourself. You know how it is."

"I know how it is," said Wilson.

"What bothers me," said Hunt, "is how anyone, even the President, knows where to take hold of a thing like this. There is no precedent. Nothing like this has ever happened before, nothing remotely like it. As a rule a crisis will build up; you can see it coming and be halfway ready for it. But not this one. This one exploded without warning."

"That's bothering me, too," said Anders. "how do you find a handle?"

"You're stuck with it," said Wilson. "You can't just ignore it. You do the best you can. You try to find out what it's all about. In a case like this, you have to be somewhat skeptical and that doesn't allow you to move as fast as you'd like to move. You have to talk with a lot of people, you have to check around and you have to develop some sort of judgment. I suspect you might pray a lot. Oh, not informal praying, nothing like that. . . ."

"Is that what the President did?" asked Anders.

"That's not what I said. I was just trying to think through a hypothetical question."

"What do you think of it, Steve?" asked Gates. "You, not the President."

"It's hard to tell," said Wilson. "It's all too new. I found myself, just a while ago, wondering if it was all delusion, if it might not be gone by morning. Of course, I know it won't be. But it boggles the mind to think of it. I have brought myself to believe these people are really from the future. But even if they're not, they're here and we have to deal with them. I suppose it doesn't really matter where they came from."

"You, personally, still have doubts?"

"You mean are they from the future? No, I don't think I have any real doubts about that. Their explanation holds up. Why

73

should they lie about it? What would they gain by lying?"

"But, still, you. . . ."

"Now, wait a minute. I don't want you to start speculating the answer that we have is wrong. That would be unrealistic. This was among friends, remember? Just sitting down and talking."

The pressroom door came open and, at the sound of its opening, Wilson looked up. Brad Reynolds stood in the doorway. His face had a pitifully stricken look.

"Steve," he said, "Steve, I have to see you."

"What's going on?" asked Hunt.

Through the open door came the frantic clanging of a bell on one of the teletypes, signaling a bulletin.

Wilson rose to his feet so swiftly that he jiggled the coffee table, tipping his cup. Coffee ran across the table and dripped onto the carpet.

He strode across the room and gripped Reynolds by the arm.

"A monster got through!" Reynolds blurted out. "Global has it. It's on radio."

"For the love of God," said Wilson. He glanced back over his shoulder at the newsmen and saw that they had heard.

"What's this about monsters?" shouted Anders. "You never told us about any monsters."

"Later," said Wilson savagely. He pushed Reynolds back into the pressroom and slammed the door.

"I thought you and Frank were working on the TV speech," he said. "How did you. . . ."

"The radio," said Reynolds. "We heard it on the radio. What will we do about the TV talk? He can't go on TV without mentioning this and it's only an hour away."

"We'll take care of that," said Wilson. "Does Henderson know?"

"Frank went to tell him. I came to you."

"Do you know what happened? Where it happened?"

"Down in Virginia. Two of them came through the tunnel. The gun got one of them. The other one got through. It killed the gun crew. . . ."

"You mean one of them is running loose?"

Reynolds nodded miserably.

22

TOM MANNING turned sideways from his desk and ran new paper into the typewriter. He wrote:

Third Lede Monster
WASHINGTON, D.C. (Global)—An alien beast is loose on the Earth tonight. No one knows where it is. It came out of a time tunnel in Virginia and disappeared after killing the crew of an artillery piece posted in front of the tunnel, placed to prevent the very thing that happened. A second beast came through with it, but this one was killed by the gun.

There are unconfirmed reports that several other people, in addition to the gun crew, were killed by the tunnel monster.

Eyewitnesses said that the beast was large and unbelievably quick in its movements. No one got a good look at it. "It moved too fast to really see it," said one eyewitness. Within seconds after emerging from the tunnel it disappeared. There is no clue as to where it may be now.

"Mr. Manning," said someone at his elbow.
Manning looked up. A copy boy stood there.
"Mr. Price's pictures," said the copy boy, handing them to him.
Manning looked at the one on top and drew his breath in sharply. "Jesus H. Christ," he said to himself aloud, "will you look at that!"

It was the sort of picture that some press flack would dream up to advertise a horror movie, but without the phoniness of such a drawing. The creature was springing, perhaps toward the gun crew, probably moving fast, for there was a sense of power and swiftness in it. Bentley's super-fast film had frozen it in all its ferocity—the bared mouthful of fangs, the talons gleaming in the fur of one uplifted paw, the nest of writhing tentacles positioned around its squat, thick neck. Its eyes shone wickedly and a thick ruff of fur around its neck stood up on end. The very shape of it was evil. It was beast, but more than beast. There was in it some quality that sent a shiver up one's spine—not a shiver of horror, but of outlandish, unreasoning, mindless fear.

Manning swung back to the desk and laid the pictures on its top. With a swipe of his hand, he fanned them out as one would fan a hand of playing cards. All of them were horrifying. A couple of them showed, somewhat less well than Manning would have liked, the shambles where the tunnel mouth had been, with the dead monster crumpled on top of the trampled human bodies.

"That goddamned Price," said Manning soulfully. "He never got a shot of the monster and the gun crew."

23

"WE can't cancel your TV appearance," Wilson told the President. "It's bad enough right now. It will be worse if we cancel your appearance. We can fix it, a paragraph or two at the start of it. Say that the Virginia incident is too recent to make much comment upon it. Assurance that it will be run down, that it will be found and killed. That we're already closing in on it. . . ."

"But we aren't," said the President. "We don't know where the hell it is. There's been no report of it. You remember what Gale said—how fast they could move. Traveling in the dark, this thing could be deep into the mountains of West Virginia and well hidden out before it's daylight."

"There's more reason right now than there ever was," said Frank Howard, who had been working on the speech text with Reynolds, "for you to talk to the people. The country, the entire country, will be in an uproar and we'll have to tame them down."

"You know, Frank," said the President, "I don't seem to care right now to tame the country down. Can't you get it through your head that this is not a political matter? It's far more than that. I can't be sure just how much danger the country may be facing, but I know that there is danger. I've asked Gale to step down here and tell us what he thinks. He knows more of it than we do."

"What you refuse to understand, sir," said Wilson, "is that the country's waiting to hear from you. They would like some sort of assurance, but if you can't give them that, you can let them know that we are on the job. Seeing and hearing you, in itself, will be visible proof that everything has not entirely gone to pot. They need some physical evidence that the government is aware of what is going on. . . ."

The box on the President's desk purred. "Yes?" said the President.

"A call for Mr. Wilson, sir, an urgent call. Can he take it there?"

The President lifted the receiver and handed to Wilson.

"This is Henry," said Hunt's voice. "Sorry for breaking in, but I thought that you should know. One of the other tunnels failed out in Wisconsin. It just came in on AP."

"Failed, you say. Not like Virginia. Nothing came through?"

"Apparently. The message said it failed. Blinked out. Wasn't there anymore."

"Thank you, Henry. Thanks for telling me."

He said to the President, "Another tunnel is out. Cut off. Disappeared. I suppose the people did it at the other end. Gale told us, you remember, they had men on guard who were prepared to collapse the tunnels if anything went wrong."

"I do recall," said the President. "The invaders must be getting at them. I don't like to think about it. It must take a lot of courage to do a thing like that. The ones at the other end of the Virginia tunnel apparently didn't have the chance to do it."

"About the speech, sir," said Reynolds. "The time is getting short."

"All right. I suppose I have to. Do the best you can. But don't say anything about having it tracked down and cornered."

"You'll have to tell them what it is," said Wilson. "There has to be an explanation of what the monster is. We'll have to tell the people it's monsters such as this the tunnel folks are fleeing."

"There'll be a scream to shut down the tunnels," Reynolds said.

"Let them scream," said the President. "We don't know of any way of shutting them except firing into them. And, without reason, we can't fire into crowds of refugees—our own refugees."

"In a short while," said Howard, "there may be no need. One tunnel has shut down of itself. There will be others of them. In a few hours, maybe, all of them."

"I hope not," said the President. "No matter what else happens, no matter what problems they may bring us, I can't help but hope all the people do get through."

Kim stuck her head in the door. "Mr. Gale is here, sir."

"OK. Send him in."

Gale came into the room. He half-stumbled as he walked across the room, then stiffened and marched up to within a few feet of the desk. His face was haggard.

"I am so sorry, sir," he said. "I can't properly express the regrets of myself or of my people. We thought we had taken safeguards."

"Please sit down, Mr. Gale," said the President. "You can help us now. We need your help."

Gale sat carefully in the chair. "You mean about the alien. You want to know more about it. I could have told you more this afternoon, but there was so much to tell and I never thought. ..."

"I'll accept your word for that. You did make provisions to guard against what happened. Perhaps you did the best you could. Now we need your help to find this creature. We need to know something about its habits, what we can expect. We have to hunt it down."

"Lucklly," said Reynolds, "there is only one of them. When we get it. ..."

"It is unfortunately," said Gale, "not as lucky as you think. The aliens are bisexual creatures. ..."

"You mean. ..."

"That's exactly what I mean," said Gale. "The young are hatched from eggs. Any of the adults can lay fertilized eggs. And lay them in great numbers. Once hatched, the young need no care, or at least are given no care and. ..."

"Then," said the President, "we must find it before it starts laying eggs."

"That is right," said Gale, "although I fear you may be too late already. From what we know of them, I would suspect that the creature would start laying eggs within a few hours after its emergence from the tunnel. It would recognize the crisis. You must, first of all, disabuse yourself of any thoughts you may have suggesting that the aliens are no more than monsters. They are a great deal more than that. They are highly intelligent. Their mental and physical processes are geared to a ritualistic violence—at least we think it's ritualistic—but that doesn't mean they're stupid. This creature knows that it's the sole representative of its species in this particular time, and it will realize, as well, that it may remain the only one, that the future of the species in this time bracket may rely upon it alone. This will not be an intellectual realization only, but I would suspect, from what I know of them, that its body will realize and respond to the situation as well and that all its physical resources will be aimed at producing eggs, as many eggs as it can manage. Furthermore, realizing that eventually it will be hunted down and slain and that the nests of eggs will be hunted as well, it will scatter its clutches of eggs over as much territory as it can. It will seek out desolate and uninhabited spots in which to make its nests, it will hide them carefully, it will locate them in the least accessible spots. It is fighting, you understand, not only for itself, but for the species. Perhaps not at all for itself, but only for the species."

The other four in the office sat in stricken silence. Finally the President stirred uneasily and spoke. "You give us no chance, then, of finding it before it has laid its eggs."

"I would think there is no chance at all," said Gale. "It probably already has laid some of them. It will continue laying them. I suppose I should give you some hope, if for no other reason than to lighten my own guilt, the guilt of my people. But it would be unfair to tell you less than truth. I am very sorry, sir."

"I would suspect," said the President, "that it might be heading for the mountains. But that supposition is based only on my knowledge there are mountains to the west."

"It would know as well," said Gale. "It has as good a geographical knowledge of this area as any of us here. The geography is the same five hundred years into the future as it is today."

"Then," said the President, "assuming that it would have

80

headed for the mountains, we must not only head it off, but we will have to give some thought to evacuating the people from that area as well."

"You're thinking nuclear," said Wilson. "Blanketing the area with bombs. You can't do that, sir. Only as a last resort and perhaps not even then. The tonnage would have to be massive and the fallout. . . ."

"You're jumping to conclusions, Steve. I agree with you—only as a last resort and perhaps not even then."

"There is one thing I must speak of," said Gale. "Do not underestimate the enemy. Either its intelligence or its ferocity. It is a killer. Even with great odds against it, it still is a killer. Now, under these circumstances, it probably will try to avoid confrontation, will run rather than fight, will try to keep itself alive to build up whatever margin it can for the survival of the species. But get it into a corner and it will strike back. You see, it doesn't mind dying. It has no fear of death."

The President nodded gravely. "I appreciate that," he said. "But there is something else."

"Anything," said Gale.

"You told us your people could supply us with specifications for the building of the tunnels."

"That is true," said Gale.

"The point is this," said the President. "If we are to do anything at all we should do it quickly. If we delay, a dangerous social and economic, not to say political, situation may build up. I am sure that you can understand this. And this matter of the monster has given us even less time than I thought we had. For that reason it seems to me important that we have the specifications and talk with your people who can explain them to us as soon as possible."

"Mr. President," said Reynolds, "we have less than two hours to get your talk shaped up."

"Certainly," said the President. "I am sorry to have held you up. Steve, you can stay a moment, please."

"Thank you, sir," said Howard, following Reynolds toward the door.

"Now, where were we?" said the President. "Oh, yes, I was saying that we need to get to work on the matter of the tunnels. I plan to have some of our physicists and engineers come in and confer with your people. . . ."

"Does that mean, sir, that you will help us?"

"I would think so, Mr. Gale, although at the moment I'm in no position to make a positive commitment. But I don't see much else that we can do. We can't keep you here. We can't possibly absorb you into our population. It would wreck our economy. The first step would seem to be to talk with your physicists and find out what's involved—what kind of fabrications we will need, what kind of engineering, how much labor. Until we know that, we can't do any planning. And there's the matter, as well, of selecting sites."

"We have that all worked out," said Gale. "Our geologists have made a study, as well as is possible, of the Miocene terrain. It would be an easy matter to have a tunnel emerge above an oceanic arm or in the middle of a lake or a volcanic area. Stable land surfaces have been pinpointed and mapped out. We can't be entirely sure, of course, but our people, operating within their best knowledge, have done at least the preliminary work."

"Then," said the President, "we won't have to worry about that. But we do need something to get started on."

"The men you want to talk with," said Gale, "were among the first to come through the tunnel. I presume they are wherever you have been taking the people who came from the Virginia tunnel."

"Fort Myer," said the President. "Or at least the most of them went there. The army set up a number of inflatable shelters."

"I can give you their names," said Gale, "but I'll have to go with whoever is sent to contact them. Without me, they'd refuse to come. You can understand our situation, sir. We could take no chances of our men or their information falling into other than official hands."

The President frowned. "I'm reluctant to let you leave, even for a short time. You can, of course, walk out of here any time you wish. You are in no way detained. But we may have need of your advice on a moment's notice. Our information so far is sketchy. You have done an excellent job of supplying us with it, of course, but situations can arise. . . ."

"I understand," said Gale. "Alice, perhaps. They know her and if she carried a note from me, on a White House letterhead. . . ."

"That would be fine," said the President, "if she would be willing. Steve, I wonder if you'd undertake to accompany her."

"Certainly, sir. But my car's not here. Judy drove it home."

"You can have a White House car and driver. Perhaps we'd better send along a Secret Service man. It may seem a silly precaution, but a lot is riding on this."

He put up his hand and made a gesture of wiping his face.

"I hope to God, Mr. Gale," he said, "that you and I, your people and our people, can work together on this. This is just the beginning of it. It's going to get rough. There'll be all sorts of pressure, all kinds of frenzied screaming. Have you got a good strong back and a good thick skin?"

"I think I have," said Gale.

24

THE Attorney General's visitor was an old and valued friend. They had been roommates at Harvard and in the years since then had kept in touch. Reilly Douglas knew that, in large part, he owed his cabinet appointment to the good offices and, perhaps, the political pressure that could be commanded by Clinton Chapman, a man who headed one of the nation's most prestigious industrial complexes and a heavy contributor to the party's funds.

"I know this must be a busy time for you," Chapman told Douglas, "and under the circumstances I'll take very little of your time."

"It's good to see a friendly face," said Douglas. "I don't mind telling you I don't go along with this. Not that there's nothing to it, for there is. But we're rushing into it. The President has accepted at face value this story of time traveling and while I can see, at the moment, no other explanation, it seems to me there should be some further study of the matter before we commit ourselves."

"Well, now," said Chapman, "I agree with you—I couldn't agree more completely with you. I called in some of my physicists this afternoon. You know, of course, that among our several branches, we have a respectable corps of research people. Well, as I was saying, I called a few of them together earlier today and we did some brain-storming on this time tunnel business. . . ."

"And they told you it was impossible."

"Not exactly that," said Chapman. "Not quite that at all. Not that any of them can see quite how it's done, but they told me, and this is something that surprised me, that the matter of the direction in which time flows and precisely why it flows that way has been a subject of some quiet study and very scholarly dispute for a number of years. They talked about a lot of things I didn't understand and used terms I'd never heard before. Arrows of time and boundary conditions, for example, and it seems that the arrows of time they talk about can be viewed from a number of different points—statistical, biological, thermodynamical, and I suppose other terms that have slipped my mind. They talked about the principle of wave retardation and causality and there was quite a lot of discussion about time-symmetrical field equations and the upshot of it all seemed to be that while, on the basis of present knowledge and research it all seems plain impossible, there is really nothing hard and fast that says it can't be done. The gate, it appears, is just a little bit ajar. Someone come along and give that gate a little push and it might be possible."

"You mean that in another hundred years or so. . . ."

Chapman nodded. "I guess that's what it means. They tried to explain some of it to me, but it didn't take. I haven't the background to understand what they were telling me. These people have a lingo of their own and so far as people like you and I may be concerned it's a foreign language we never knew existed."

"So it could be true," said Douglas. "On the face of what is happening, it quite clearly is true. There seems no other explanation, but my point was that we should not move until we know it's true. And, personally, while I could think of no other explanations, I found a great deal of difficulty in believing it."

"Just exactly what," asked Chapman, "is the government thinking about doing? Building new tunnels, I understand, and sending the people of the future still farther back in time. Do they have any idea of what it's going to cost? Or how much time it might take? Or. . . ."

"They have no idea," said Douglas. "Not a single figure. No inkling of what's involved. But if anything can be done, we will have to do it. The people from the future can't be kept here. It would be impossible to do it. Somehow we must get rid of them."

"My hunch," said Chapman, "is that it will cost a bundle. And there'll be hell's own uproar about the cost of it. The public is more tax-conscious than it has ever been and something like this could bring about a confiscatory tax."

"You're getting at something, Clint."

"Yes, I suppose I am. A gamble, you might say."

"You always gambled well," said Douglas. "You have a natural poker face."

"It's going to cost a lot of money," Chapman said.

"Tax money," Douglas said.

"I know. Tax money. And that could mean we'd lose the election a year from now. You know I've always been rather generous in my campaign contributions and have very rarely asked for favors. I'm not asking for one now. But under certain circumstances, I would be willing to make what I might think of as a somewhat more substantial contribution. Not only to the party, but to the country."

"That would be very generous of you," said Douglas, not entirely sure that he was happy with the turn the talk had taken.

"I'd have to have some figures and some facts, of course," said Chapman, "but unless the cost is higher than I could manage, I think I would be agreeable to taking over the construction of the tunnels. That is, if the tunnels can be built."

"In return for which?"

"In return for which," said Chapman, "I should like exclusive future license for the building of tunnels and the operation of them."

Douglas frowned. "I don't know," he said. "I can't be certain of the legality of an arrangement of that sort. And there is the international angle. . . ."

"If you applied yourself to it," said Chapman, "you could figure out a way. I am sure you could. You're a damn good lawyer, Reilly."

"There must be something I am missing. I don't see why you should want the license. What good would the tunnels be?"

"After all of this is over," Chapman said, "people will be

considerably intrigued with the idea of traveling in time. A brand new way of traveling. A way of getting places they could never get before."

"But that's insane!"

"Not as insane as you might think. Imagine what a sportsman would be willing to pay for the privilege of going back to prehistoric days for a spot of hunting. Universities would want to send teams of paleontologists back to the Age of Reptiles to study and photograph the dinosaurs. Classical historians would sell their souls to go back and learn what really happened at the siege of Troy. . . ."

"And the church," said Douglas rather acidly, "might want a first-class ticket for a seat at the Crucifixion."

"I suppose that, too," Chapman agreed, "and, as you imply, there would be times when it might get slightly sticky. There'd have to be rules and regulations worked out and certain safeguards set up not to change the course of history, but. . . ."

"It wouldn't work," said Douglas flatly. "Time traveling, we are told, works in only one direction, back toward the past. Once you go back, you can't return. You can't move future-ward."

"I'm not so sure of that," said Chapman. "Maybe that's what you were told. Maybe that's true now. But my physicists assured me this afternoon that if you can move in time at all, you can move in both directions. They were sure of that. Sure it could be worked out. It simply makes no sense, they said, for the flow to go only one way. If you can go into the past, you certainly can go futureward, for that would seem the preferred direction. That's what we have right now."

"Clint, I can't go along on this."

"You can think about it. You can see how things develop. You can keep me well informed. If it should work out, there would be something very worthwhile in it for you."

25

"SO now you'll explain to me, perhaps," said Alice Gale, "what a picnic is. You told me this afternoon you had been going on a picnic."

The Secret Service man hunched forward on the seat. "Has Steve been talking picnic to you? Don't ever chance it with him. . , ."

"But, Mr. Black," she said, "I don't even know what a picnic is."

"It's fairly simple," Wilson told her. "You pack a lunch and you go out in a park or woods and you eat it there."

"But we did that up in our time," she said. "Although we did not call it picnic. I don't think we called it anything at all. I never heard it called anything at all."

The car rolled slowly down the drive, heading for the gate. The driver, in the seat up front, sat erect and straight. The car slowed to a halt and a soldier came up to the driver's window. There were other military men stationed by the gate.

"What is going on?" asked Wilson. "I had not heard of this."

Black shrugged. "Someone got the wind up. This place is closed in tight. It's stiff with military. There are mortars scattered through the park and no one knows what else."

"Does the President know about it?"

"I'm not sure," said Black. "No one might have thought to tell him."

The soldier stepped back and the gate came open and the car went through. It proceeded silently along the street, heading for the bridge.

Wilson peered out the window. "Where is everyone?" he asked. "A Sunday night and the tourist season and there's no one here."

"You heard the news," said Black.

"Of course I heard the news."

"Everyone's holed up. Everyone's indoors. They expect a monster to come leaping out at them."

"We had such lovely places we could go out on picnics," said Alice Gale. "So many parks, so much wild land. More open spaces than you have. Not as crowded as you have it now, although somehow I like it crowded. There are so many people; there is so much to see."

"You are enjoying it," said Wilson.

"Yes, of course, enjoying it. Although I have the feel of guilt in my enjoyment. My father and I should be with our people. But I was telling you of our time. It was a good time to live in. Until the aliens came, of course. And even then part of the time, in the earlier days, before there were so many of them. They were not at our throats all the time, you know, except in the last few years. Although I don't think we ever were unaware of them. We always talked about them. We never really forgot them, no matter what. All my life, I think, they have been in my mind. There were times, in the later years, when we were obsessed with them. We continually looked over our shoulders to see if they were there; we were never free of them. We talked of them and studied them. . . ."

"You say you studied them," said Wilson. "Exactly how did you study them? Who studied them?"

"Why," she said, "biologists, of course. At times they came into possession of an alien's body. And the psychologists and psychiatrists, as well. The evolutionists. . . ."

"Evolutionists?"

"Certainly, evolutionists. For these aliens were very strange evolutionarily. They seemed to be creatures that were consciously in control of their evolutionary processes. There are times when you are inclined to suspect they can order their evolutionary processes. My father, I think, explained some of this to you. In all their long history of evolution they apparently gave up no evolutionary advantage they had gained. They made no compromises, trading one thing for another. They kept what they had and needed and added whatever else they could develop. This, of course, means they are adaptive creatures. They can adapt to almost any condition or situation. They respond almost instantly to stresses and emergencies. . . ."

"You almost sound," said Black, "as if you—well, not you, perhaps, but your people—might admire these creatures."

She shook her head. "We hated them and feared them. That is quite apparent, for we ran away from them. But, yes, I suppose we might have felt something like awed admiration, although we did not admit it. I don't think anyone ever said it."

"Lincoln is coming up ahead," said Wilson. "Naturally, you know Lincoln."

"Yes," she said. "My father has Lincoln's bedroom."

The memorial loomed ahead, softly lit against the night-black sky. The statue sat deep within the recess, brooding in the marble chair.

The car moved past and the memorial was left behind.

"If we can find the time," said Wilson, "in the next few days, we'll go out and see it. Or, perhaps, you may have seen it. But you said the White House. . . ."

"The memorial, too," she said. "Part of it is left, but less than half it it. The stones are fallen down."

"What is this?" asked Black.

"Up in the time the people of the tunnel came from," said Wilson, "Washington had been destroyed. The White House is a wilderness."

"But that's impossible. I don't understand. A war?"

"Not a war," said Alice Gale. "It's hard to explain, even if you know it and I have little understanding of it—I have read little of it. Economic collapse, perhaps, is the best name for it. Probably some ethical collapse as well. A time of mounting inflation that reached ridiculous heights, matched by a mounting cynicism, a loss of faith in government, which contributed to the failure of government, a growing gap of resources and understanding between the rich and poor. It all grew up and up and then it all collapsed. Not this nation only, but all the major powers. One after one they fell. The economy was gone and government was gone and mobs ran in the street. Blind mobs striking out, not at anything in particular, but at anything at all. You must excuse me, please; I tell it very badly."

"And this is all ahead of us?" asked Black.

"Not now," said Wilson. "Not any more it isn't. Or at least it doesn't have to be. We're on a different time track now."

"You," said Black, "are as bad as she is. You don't, either one, make sense."

"I'm sorry, Mr. Black," said Alice.

"Don't mind me," said Black. "I'm not the intellectual sort. I'm just an educated cop. Steve will tell you that."

26

THE Reverend Dr. Angus Windsor was a good man. He stood in grace and was distinguished in good works. He was pastor of a church that had its roots in wealth, a long history and a certain elegance and yet this did not prevent him from going where the need was greatest—outside his own parish, certainly, for in that particular parish there was little need. He was seen in the ghettos and he was present where the young demonstration marchers fell beneath the rain of clubs wielded by police. When he heard of a family that had need of food he showed up at the door with a bag of groceries and before he left managed to find a few dollars in his pockets that he could get along without. He was a regular visitor at prisons, and the lonely old folks put away to die in rest homes were familiar with his stately tread, his stooped shoulders, his long white hair and patient face. That he was not at all averse to good publicity, sometimes even seemed to court it, was held against him by some of the influential members of his congregation, who subscribed to the belief that this characteristic was unseemly in him, but he went his way with no attention paid to this criticism; once he was supposed to have told an old, dear friend that it was a small price to pay for the privilege of doing good—although whether he meant the publicity or the criticism was not entirely clear.

So it was thought by the newsmen present not at all unusual when, late in the evening, he appeared at the site where the tunnel had been closed upon the emergence of the monsters.

The newsmen clustered around the old man.

"What are you doing here, Dr. Windsor?" asked one of them.

"I came," said Dr. Angus, "to offer to these poor souls the small shreds of comfort it is in my power to dispense. I had a slight amount of trouble with the military. I understand they are letting no one in. But I see they let you people in."

"Some of us talked our way in. Others parked a mile or so away and walked."

"The good Lord interceded for me," said Dr. Angus, "and they let me through the barricade."

"How did He intercede for you?"

"He softened their hearts toward me and then they let me go. But now I must speak to these poor folks."

He motioned at the scattered groups of refugees standing in the yards and along the street.

The dead monster lay upon its back, with its clawed feet sticking in the air and its limp tentacles lying snakelike along the ground. Most of the human bodies at the tunnel mouth had been moved. A few still lay here and there, shadowed lumps upon the grass, covered by blankets. The gun lay where it had been toppled on its side.

"The army is sending out a team," said one of the newsmen, "to haul in the monster. They want to have a good look at him."

The spotlights mounted in the trees cast a ghastly radiance over the area where the tunnel mouth had lain. Off in the darkness the generator engine coughed and sputtered. Trucks pulled in, loaded up and left. On occasion the bullhorn still roared out its orders.

Dr. Windsor, with an instinct born of long practice, headed unerringly for the largest group of refugees, huddled at an intersection beneath a swaying streetlamp. Most of them were standing on the pavement, but others sat upon the curbs and there were small groups of them scattered on the lawns.

Dr. Windsor came up to a group of women—he always zeroed in on women; they were more receptive to his particular brand of Christianity than were men.

"I have come," he said, making a conscious effort to hold down his pomposity, "to offer you the comfort of the Lord. In times like this, we should always turn to Him."

The women stared at him in some amazement. Some of them instinctively backed away.

"I'm the Reverend Windsor," he told them, "and I came from Washington. I go where I am called. I go to meet a need. I wonder, would you pray with me?"

A tall, slender grandmotherly woman stepped to the forefront of the group. "Please go away," she said.

Dr. Windsor fluttered his hands, stricken off balance. "But I don't understand," he said. "I only meant. . . ."

"We know what you meant," the woman told him, "and we thank you for the thought. We know it was only kindness in you."

"You can't mean what you are saying," said Dr. Windsor, who, by now, was flustered. "You cannot hope, by your word alone, to deprive all the others. . . ."

A man came thrusting through the crowd and seized the pastor by the arm. "My friend," he said, "let us keep it down."

"But this woman. . . ."

"I know. I heard what you said to her. It is not her choice only. She speaks for the rest of us."

"I fail to understand."

"There is no need for you to understand. Now will you please go."

"You reject me?"

"Not you, sir. Not personally. We reject the principle you stand for."

"You reject Christianity?"

"Not Christianity alone. In the Logic Revolution of a century ago, we rejected all religions. Our non-belief is as firm a faith as is your belief. We do not thrust our principles on you. Will you please not thrust yours on us?"

"This is incredible," said the Reverend Dr. Windsor. "I can't believe my ears. I will not believe it. There must be some mistake. I had only meant to join with you in prayer."

"But, parson, we no longer pray."

Dr. Windsor turned about, went blundering up the street, toward the waiting newsmen, who had trailed after him. He shook his head, bewildered. It was unbelievable. It could not be right. It was inconceivable. It was blasphemous.

After all the years of man's agony, after all the searching for the truth, after all the saints and martyrs, it could not come to this!

27

GENERAL DANIEL FOOTE, commandant at Fort Myer, was waiting for them with the three men in his office.

"You should not have come alone," he said to Wilson. "I said so to the President, but he would not listen. I offered to send an escort, but he vetoed the idea. He said he wanted to draw no attention to the car."

"There was little traffic on the road," said Wilson.

The commandant shook his head. "These are unsettled times," he said.

"General Foote, may I present Miss Alice Gale. Her father is the man who contacted us."

The general said, "I am glad to make your acquaintance, Miss Gale. These three gentlemen have told me something of your father. And Mr. Black. I'm glad you are along with them."

"Thank you, sir," said Black.

"I should like the privilege," Alice said, "of introducing my own people. Dr. Hardwicke, Dr. Nicholas Hardwicke, Mr. Wilson, Mr. Black. Dr. Hardwicke is a sort of Albert Einstein of our time."

The big, ungainly, bear-like man smiled at her. "You must not praise me unduly, my dear," he said. "They'll expect far too much of me. Gentlemen, I am very pleased to be here and to meet you. It is time we were getting on in this matter which must be somewhat unpleasant to you. I am glad to see you reacting so promptly and so positively. Your president must be a most unusual man.''

"We think so," Wilson said.

"Dr. William Cummings," said Alice. "Dr. Hardwicke was a fellow townsman of ours, but Dr. Cummings came from the Denver region. My father and the others thought it would be best if he were with Dr. Hardwicke when they met your scientists."

Cummings was a shrimp—small, bald, with a wrinkled, elfin face. "I am glad to be here," he said. "We all are glad to be here. We must tell you how deeply we regret what happened at the tunnel."

"And, finally," said Alice, "Dr. Abner Osborne. He is a longtime family friend."

Osborne put an arm about the girl's shoulders and hugged her. "These other gentlemen," he said, "are physicists, but I'm a more lowly creature. I am a geologist. Tell me, my dear, how is your father? I looked for him after we came through, but couldn't seem to find him."

The commandant plucked at Wilson's sleeve and the press secretary moved to one side with him.

"Tell me," said General Foote, "what you know of the monster."

"We've heard nothing further. We have assumed it would head for the mountains."

Foote nodded. "I think you may be right. We have had a few reports. Not reports, really. More like rumors. They all came from the west. Harpers Ferry. Strasburg. Luray. They must be wrong. Nothing could travel that fast. Are you absolutely sure there was only one of them?"

"You should know," said Wilson, curtly. "Your men were there. Our report was that one was killed. The other got away."

"Yes, yes, I know," said Foote. "We are bringing in the dead one."

The general was upset, thought Wilson. He was jittery. Was there something he knew that the White House did not know?

"Are you trying to tell me something, General?"

"No. Not at all," he said.

The son of a bitch, Wilson told himself. All he was doing was trying to wangle something straight out of the White House. Something that, at some later time, he could talk about when he was sitting in the officers' club.

"I think," said Wilson, "that we had best get started."

Outside they got into the car, Black in front with the driver, Wilson and Osborne on the jump seats.

"You may think it strange," said Osborne, "that there's a geologist in the group."

"I had wondered," Wilson said. "Not that you aren't welcome."

"It was thought," said Osborne, "that there might be some questions about the Miocene."

"About us going there, you mean. About us going back as well as you."

"It is one way in which the problem could be solved."

"Are you trying to tell me that you were fairly sure some of the monsters would get through? That enough of them might get through that we'd be forced to leave?"

"Certainly not," said the geologist. "We had hoped none would get through. We'd set up precautions. I can't imagine what could have happened. I'm not inclined to think that this single monster. . . ."

"But you don't know."

"You're right. They're monstrous clever things. Very capable. Some of our biologists could tell you more."

"Then why this feeling we should go back into the Miocene?"

"You're nearing a danger point," said Osborne. "Our historians could explain it better than I can, but all the signs are there. Oh, I know that now you've been switched over to a different time track and will travel a different road than we. But I think that the changeover may have come too late."

"What you're talking about is the economic and social collapse. Alice told us Washington, up in your time, is gone. I suppose New York, as well, and Chicago and all the rest. . . ."

"You're top-heavy," said Osborne. "You've gotten out of balance. I think it's gone too far to stop. You have a runaway economy and the social cleavages are getting deeper by the day and. . . ."

"And going back to the Miocene would put an end to it?"

"It would be a new start."

"I'm not so sure," said Wilson.

Up in the front, Black raised his voice. "It's time for the President's speech. Shall I turn on the radio?"

He didn't wait for anyone to say he should. He turned it on.

The President was talking.

". . . little I can tell you. So I shall not keep you long. We still are in the process of sorting out the facts and I would be doing you a disservice if I told you less, or more, than facts. You may be assured that your government will level with you. As soon as we know anything for certain, you shall know it, too. We'll pass it on to you.

"These things we do know. Up in the future, some five hundred years from now, our descendants were attacked by an alien race. For twenty years or more our people held them off, but it became apparent that they could not stand against them indefinitely. Retreat was called for, but there was only one place they could retreat. Quite fortunately, they had been able to develop time travel and so it was possible for them to retreat in time. This they did, coming back to us. They do not intend to stay here; as soon as possible they intend to go back, far deeper into time. But to do this they need our help. Not only our help in building the time tunnels they will need, but our help in supplying the bare basics which will enable them to start over again. For economic reasons which everyone must understand, we, in conjunction with the rest of the world, cannot refuse to help them. Not that we would refuse in any case. They are our children's children, several times removed. They are our flesh and blood and we cannot withhold assistance. How we will go about the helping of them is now under consideration There are problems and they must and will be solved. There must be no delay and our effort must be wholehearted. It will call for sacrifice and devotion from every one of you. There are many details which you should be told, many questions which must occur to you. These all will be fully given and fully answered later; there is not the time to put them all before you this evening. After all, this all began happening only a few hours ago. It has been a busy Sunday."

The voice was confident, resonant, with no hint of desperation—and, thought Wilson, there must be in the man a certain sense of desperation. But he was still the old competent campaigner, the polished politician. He still could sell himself, still could reassure the nation. Hunched forward on the jump seat, Wilson felt a sudden surge of pride in him.

"All of you know by now," the President was saying, "that two of the aliens came through a tunnel in Virginia. One of them was killed, the other one escaped. I must be honest with you and say that we have had no subsequent word of it. We are pressing all efforts to find and destroy it and while it may take a little time, we will do exactly that. I ask you most urgently not to place too much emphasis upon the fact that an alien is loose upon the Earth. It is only one of the many problems that we face tonight, and not the most important. Given the sort of cooperation that I know we can expect from you, we will solve them all."

He paused and for a moment Wilson wondered if that was all—although he knew it wasn't all, for the President had not said good night.

The voice took up again. "I have one unpleasant thing to say and, unpleasant as it may be, I know that, on due consideration, you'll realize that it must be done, that it is the least that I can do. You'll realize, I think, that it is necessary for the good of all of us. I have, just a few minutes ago, signed an executive order declaring a national emergency. Under that order, a bank and trading holiday has been declared. This means that no banks or other financial institutions will open their doors for business, or transact any business, until further notice. Under the order all trading in stocks, shares and bonds, or in any commodities, will be suspended until further notice. All prices, salaries and wages will be frozen. This, of course, is an intolerable situation and cannot exist for long. Because of this, it is only an emergency order that will be lifted as soon as the Congress and other branches of the government can implement rules and regulations imposing such restraints as are necessary under the situation which has been imposed upon us. I hope that you will bear with us over the few days the executive order will be in force. It was only with the utmost reluctance that I decided it was necessary."

Wilson let out his breath slowly, not realizing until he let it out that he had caught and held it.

There'd be unsheeted hell to pay, he knew. From the country and from the White House press corps. For Christ's sake, Steve, you could have tipped us off. You could have let us know. And they would not believe him when he told them he had not known himself.

It was such a logical step that they should have guessed it; he, himself, should have thought of it. But he hadn't. He wondered if the President had talked it over with anyone and he doubted that he had. There hadn't been much time and there'd been other things he had to talk about.

The President was saying good night to his listeners.

"Good night, Mr. President," said Wilson, and wondered why the others looked at him so strangely.

28

THE pressroom office was dark except for the feeble light from the clacking wire machines ranged along the wall. Wilson crossed to his desk and sat down. He leaned forward to snap on the desk lamp, then pulled back his hand. There was no need of light and there was healing in the dark. He leaned back in his chair; for the first time since this afternoon there was nothing he should do, but there was still inside him the nagging sense that he should be up and doing.

The President, he thought, should long since be in bed. It was nearly midnight and well past his usual bedtime and he had missed his nap in the afternoon. Samuel Henderson, he thought, was getting old, too old for this sort of thing. He had seemed drawn and haggard when the refugee scientists were escorted to his office to be introduced to the men from the National Academy.

"You heard my speech, Steve?" the President had asked him when the men were gone.

"In the car."

"What do you think? Will the country go along?"

"Not at first. Not willingly. But when they think about it, I believe they will. Wall Street will raise a lot of dust."

"Wall Street," said the President, "is something I can't afford to give my time to right now."

"You should be heading for bed, Mr. President. It's been a long, hard day."

"Directly," said the President. "First I have to talk with Treasury and Sandburg phoned in to ask if he could come over."

Directly, he had said, but it still would be hours, more than likely, before he got to sleep.

Somewhere, in some secret room, the scientists were talking; out there, in the vastness of the nation, of the world, in fact, people from the future were walking from their tunnels; in the mountains to the west a monster was skulking in the darkness.

It still was unbelievable. It had happened all too fast. A man had not been given time to catch up with it. In a few hours now the people would be waking to a new day that, in many respects, would be utterly unlike any day before, unlike any day in all of human history, faced by problems and dilemmas no man had ever faced before.

Light showed through the crack underneath the doors that led into the press lounge. Some members of the press would still be there, although they were not working. There was no sound of typewriters. He remembered that he'd never gotten to eat the sandwiches. He'd put two of them upon a plate and had taken a bite out of one of them when Brad Reynolds had come bursting through the door. Now that he thought of it, he realized that he was hungry. There might be some sandwiches left, although they'd be dry by now, and for some reason, he wanted to stay here in the dark, alone, with no necessity of talking to anyone at all.

Although, perhaps, he thought, he should see what was on the wires. He sat for a moment longer, unwilling to move, then got up and went across the room to the bank of teletypes. AP first, he thought. Good, old stolid AP. Never sensational, usually fairly solid.

Yards of copy had been fed out of the machine, running down into wads of folded paper back of the machine.

A new story was just starting. . . .

WASHINGTON (AP)—A search is being pressed tonight in the mountains west of here for the monster that escaped from a time tunnel in Virginia a few hours ago. There have been numerous reports of sightings, but none can be confirmed. There is reason to believe that most of them arose from fertile and concerned imaginations. A number of troops and contingents from many police and sheriff's departments are being deployed into the area, but there is little hope that a great deal can be done before daylight. . . .

Wilson hauled in the copy paper, letting it fall and curl up before his feet, checking rapidly.

LONDON, ENGLAND (AP)—As dawn came this morning ministers still were in conference at the residence of the Prime Minister. Throughout the night, there had been a steady coming and going. . . .

NEW DELHI, INDIA (AP)—For the last ten hours people and wheat have continued to pour out of the tunnels from the future. Both present problems. . . .

NEW YORK, N.Y. (AP)—Evidences multiplied throughout the night that dawn may bring an explosion of protest and rioting, not only in Harlem, but in many of the other minority areas of the city. Fear that the heavy influx of refugees from the future may bring about a reduction in food allotments and other welfare benefits are expected to spark widespread demonstrations. All police leaves have been canceled and the police force has been notified that its personnel must be prepared to work around the clock. . . .

WASHINGTON, D.C. (AP)—The President's action declaring a business holiday and freezing wages and prices was both attacked and praised. . . .

Moscow, Madrid, Singapore, Brisbane, Bogota, Cairo, Kiev—and then:

NASHVILLE, TENN. (AP)—The Rev. Jake Billings, noted evangelist, today called for a crusade to "bring the people of the future back into the arms of Christ."

He issued the call from his headquarters here after learning that a group of refugees who had come through the now-closed time tunnel near Falls Church, Va., had refused the ministrations of the Rev. Dr. Angus Windsor, a celebrated churchman of Washington, D.C., giving as their reason that they had turned their backs, not on Christianity alone, but on all religion.

"They came to us for help," said the Rev. Billings, "but the help that they are seeking is not the help they should be given. Rather than helping them, as they ask, to go further back in time, we should help them to return to the brotherhood of Christ. They are fleeing from the future for their lives, but they have already lost a thing far more precious than their lives. How their rejection of Christ may have come about, I have no way of knowing; I do know that it is our duty to point out to them the road of devotion and of righteousness. I call upon all Christians to join me in my prayers for them."

* * *

Wilson let the long sheaf of paper fall and went back to his desk. He switched on the light and picking up the phone, dialed the switchboard.

"Jane—I thought I recognized your voice. This is Steve Wilson. Will you put in a call to Nashville for the Reverend Jake Billings? Yes, Jane, I know what time it is. I know he probably is asleep; we'll simply have to wake him up. No, I don't know his number. Thank you, Jane. Thank you very much."

He settled back in the chair and growled at himself. When he'd talked with the President early in the afternoon, Jake Billings had been mentioned and he'd promised he would call him, then it had not crossed his mind again. But who in hell would have thought a thing like this would happen?

Windsor, he thought. It would take an old busybody, a meddling fool like Windsor to go messing into it. To go messing into it and then when he got his face pushed in, to go bawling to the newsmen, telling what had happened.

Christ, that's all we need, he thought, to get the Windsors and the Billings of the country all mixed up in it, wringing their hands in pious horror and crying for a crusade. A crusade, he grimly told himself, was the last thing that was needed. There was trouble enough without a gang of pulpit thumpers adding to the dust-up.

The phone tinkled at him and he picked up the receiver. Jane said, ''The Reverend Mr. Billings is on the line, sir.''

''Hello,'' said Wilson. ''Is this the Reverend Billings?''

''Yes, God bless you,'' said the deep, solemn voice. ''What can I do for you?''

''Jake, this is Steve Wilson.''

''Wilson? Oh, yes, the press secretary. I should have known that it was you. They didn't say who was calling. They just said the White House.''

The bastard, Wilson told himself. He's disappointed. He thought it was the President.

''It's been a long time, Jake,'' he said.

''Yes,'' said Billings. ''How long ago? Ten years?''

''More like fifteen,'' said Wilson.

''I guess it is, at that,'' said Billings. ''The years do have the habit. . . .''

''I'm calling you,'' said Wilson, ''about this crusade you're drumming up.''

''Crusade? Oh, you mean the one to get the future people back onto the track. I am so glad you called. We need all the help that we can get. I view it as fortunate that they came back to us, for whatever reason. When I think of the human race, a mere five hundred years from now, forsaking the good old human faith, the faith that has sustained us all these years, I get a cold shiver up my spine. I'm so glad that you are with us. I can't tell you how glad I am that you. . . .''

''I'm not with you, Jake.''

''You're not with us? What do you mean, you're not with us?''

''I'm not with you, Jake—that is what I mean. I'm calling to ask that you call this silly crusade off.''

''But I can't. . . .''

''Yes, you can. We have trouble enough without some damn fool crusade. You'll be doing the country a disservice if you keep it up. We have problems up to here and we don't need any more. This isn't just a situation that will allow Jake Billings to show off his piety. This is life and death, not only for the refugees, but for every one of us.''

''It seems to me, Steve, you're using an approach that is unnecessarily rough.''

"If I am," said Wilson, "it's because I'm upset at what you're doing. This is important, Jake. We have a job—to get the refugees back to where they want to go before they upset our economy. And while we do that we'll be getting plenty of flak. We're going to get it from industry, from labor, from people on welfare, from politicians who will grab the chance to take cheap shots at us. With all of this, we can't face flak from you. What difference can it possibly make to you? You're not dealing with a present situation, a present people. You are dealing with the future, with a segment of time that ordinarily would be out of your reach. The refugees are back here, sure, but the windmill you are tilting at wasn't even built until long after you and I were dead."

"God moves," said Billings, "in many mysterious ways. . . ."

"Look," said Wilson, "climb down off your pulpit. Someone else, maybe, but not me. You're not going to impress me, Jake. You never did."

"Steve, are you calling for the President?"

"If you mean did he ask me to make this call, the answer is no. He probably doesn't know as yet what you have done. But when he finds out about it, he is going to be sore. The two of us talked about you earlier in the day. We were afraid you might take some sort of hand in this. We couldn't, of course, foresee what happened. But you do take a hand in everything that happens. I was supposed to phone you, to head you off beforehand. But so many things were happening, I never found the time."

"I can see your position," said Billings soberly. "I think I can even understand it. But you and I see things from different viewpoints. To me the thought that the human race became a godless people is a personal agony. It goes against everything I have been taught, everything I've lived by, all that I've believed in."

"You can rest easy," Wilson said. "It will go no further. The human future is ending, up there five hundred years ahead."

"But they'll be going back in time. . . ."

"We hope they will," said Wilson bitterly. "They'll go back, if we aren't completely hogtied by people such as you."

"If they go back," protested Billings, "they'll make a new

start. We'll give them what they need to make a new start. Into a new land and a new time where they'll build a godless culture. They may, in time, go out in space, out to other stars, and they'll go as godless people. We can't allow that, Steve.''

"Maybe you can't. I could. It wouldn't bother me. There are a hell of a lot of other people it wouldn't bother, either. You're blind if you can't see the beginning, the roots of their rejection of religion in the present. Maybe that is what is really bugging you. You're asking yourself if there was anything you could have done to prevent its happening.''

"That may be it,'' Billings admitted. "I haven't had the time to think it through. Even if it were true, it would make no difference. I still would have to do exactly what I'm doing.''

"You mean you intend to go ahead? Even knowing what it means to all of us. Stirring up the people, riding that great white horse. . . .''

"I have to do it, Steve. My conscience. . . .''

"You'll think it over? I can call again?''

For there was no use arguing further. No point in trying to talk reason to this pious madman. He'd known him, Wilson reminded himself, ever since their undergraduate years. And he should have known from the very first that it would be useless to try to make him see another point of view.

"Yes, call again,'' said Billings, "if you wish. But I won't reconsider. I know what I must do. You cannot persuade me otherwise.''

"Good night, Jake. Sorry that I woke you up.''

"You didn't wake me up. I expect no sleep this night. It was good to hear your voice, Steve.''

Wilson hung up and sat quietly in his chair. Maybe, he thought, if he'd done it differently, if he'd not come on so strong, he might have accomplished something. Although he doubted it. There was no such thing as talking reason to the man; there had never been. Perhaps if he'd called him this afternoon, after he first had talked with the President, he might have been able at least to moderate Billing's action, but he doubted that as well. It had been, he told himself, a hopeless business from the start. Billings himself was hopeless.

He looked at his watch. It was almost two o'clock. Picking up the phone, he dialed Judy's number. Her sleepy voice answered.

"Did I wake you up?"

"No, I've been waiting for you. Steve, you're awful late. What happened?"

"I had to go to Myer and pick up some refugees. Scientists. They're here, talking to the Academy people. I won't make it, Judy."

"You're not coming out?"

"I should stay in touch. There's too much happening."

"You'll be dead on your feet, come morning."

"I'll stretch out on a couch in the lounge and get some rest."

"I could come down. Stand watch."

"No need of it. Someone will get hold of me if I'm needed. You go to bed. Be a little late if you want. I can get along."

"Steve?"

"Yes?"

"It's not going good, is it?"

"It's too soon to tell."

"I saw the President on TV. It'll be an awful mess. We've never faced anything like this before."

"No, not quite like this before."

"I'm scared, Steve."

"So am I," said Wilson. "It'll be different in the morning. We'll feel different in the morning."

"I have a terrible feeling," Judy said. "As if the solid ground were slipping out beneath my feet. I've been thinking about my mother and sister out in Ohio. I haven't seen Mom in a long, long time."

"Phone her. Talk with her. You'll feel better."

"I tried to. I tried and tried. But the circuits are jammed. Everyone is calling everyone. Like a holiday. The country is upset."

"I just made a long-distance call."

"Sure you did. You're the White House. They'd clear the lines for you."

"You can call her tomorrow. Things will quiet down tomorrow."

"Steve, you're sure you can't come out? I need you."

"Sorry, Judy. Truly sorry. I have this horrible feeling that I should stay in reach. I don't know why, but I do."

"I'll see you in the morning, then."

"Try to get some sleep."

"You, too. Try to shut this out, try to get some sleep. You'll need it. Tomorrow will be bad."

They said good night and he put the receiver back into its cradle. He wondered why he was staying here. There was, at the moment, no real need to stay. Although one could never know. Hell could break loose any time.

He should try to get some sleep, he told himself, but somehow he resisted sleep. He didn't need it; he was too strung out, too tense to sleep. Later he'd need sleep, when there was no chance of sleep. Later, a few hours from now, it would all catch up with him. But right now his nerves were too tight, his brain too busy to allow for sleep.

He went out the door and around the walk to the front lawn. The night was soft, resting for the heat and turmoil of the coming day. The city was quiet. Far off a motor growled, but there were no cars on the avenue. The pillars of the portico gleamed softly in the night. The sky was clear and a million stars hung there. A red light went blinking across the sky and from far overhead came the thrum of motors.

A dark figure stirred at the edge of a group of trees.

"You all right, sir?" a voice asked.

"Yes," said Wilson. "Just out for a breath of air."

He saw now that the dark figure was a soldier, his rifle held aslant his chest.

"Don't go wandering," said the soldier. "There are a lot of us out here. Some of the boys might be a little nervous."

"I won't," said Wilson. "I'll go back in directly."

He stood listening to the quietness of the city, feeling the softness of the night. It was not the same, he told himself; there was something different. Despite the quiet and softness, a certain tenseness seemed to reach out to touch him.

29

A sound brought Elmer Ellis out of a sound sleep, sitting up in bed, befuddled, unable for a moment to orient himself. On the night table beside the bed, the clock was ticking loudly and beside him his wife, Mary, was levering herself up on her elbows.

Her sleepy voice asked, "What is it, Elmer?"

"Something's at the chickens," he said, for now the reason for his waking came churning up into his consciousness.

The sound came again, the frightened, flapping, squawking of the chickens. He threw the covers back and his feet hit the cold floor so hard it hurt.

He groped for his trousers, found them, got his legs into them, pulled them up, slid his feet into his shoes, did not stop to tie the laces. The squawking still went on.

"Where is Tige?" asked Mary.

"Damn dog," he growled. "He's off chasing possum."

He charged out the bedroom door and into the kitchen Groping, he found the shotgun, lifted it down off the pegs. From the game bag that hung beneath the pegs, he got a handful of shells, jammed them in a pocket, found two more and thrust them into the chambers of the double barrel.

Bare feet pattered toward him. "Here's the flashlight, Elmer. You can't see a thing without it."

She thrust it at him and he took it.

It was pitch black outside and he switched on the light to see his way down the porch steps. The squawking in the henhouse continued and there was no sign of Tige.

Although it was strange. In a flare of anger, he had said the dog was out hunting possum and that couldn't be true. Tige never went out hunting on his own. He was too old and stiff in the joints and he loved his bed underneath the porch.

"Tige," he said, not too loudly.

The dog whined from underneath the porch.

"What the hell is wrong with you?" asked Elmer. "What is out there, boy?"

Suddenly, he was afraid—more afraid than he'd ever been before. Even more afraid than that time he had run into the Vietcong ambush. A different kind of fear—like a cold hand reaching out and gripping him and holding him and knowing he'd never get away.

The dog whined again.

"Come on, boy," said Elmer. "Come on out and get them."

Tige did not come out.

"All right, then," said Elmer. "Stay there."

He went across the farmyard, shining his light ahead of him, picking out the henhouse door.

The frightened squawking was louder than ever now, insane and frantic.

Long ago, he told himself, he should have repaired the henhouse, plugging up the holes. With the shape that it was in, a fox would have no trouble gaining entry. Although it was strange, if it were a fox, that it should still be there. At the first flash of light, the first sound of a human voice, a fox would have been gone. A weasel, maybe, or a mink. Even a raccoon.

Outside the door he paused, reluctant to go on. But he couldn't turn back now. He'd never be able to live with himself if he did. Why, he wondered, should he be so frightened? It was Tige, he thought. Tige was so scared that he refused to come from beneath the porch, and some of that fright had rubbed off on him.

"Damn that dog," he said.

He reached out and lifted the latch, slammed the door back against the side of the building. He balanced the gun in his right hand and directed the flash with his left.

The first thing he saw in the circle of light were fea-

thers—feathers floating in the air. Then the running, squawking, flapping chickens and in among the chickens. . . .

Elmer Ellis dropped the flash and screamed and in midscream jerked the gun to his shoulder and fired blindly into the henhouse, first the right barrel, then the left, the shots so close together that they sounded as one explosion.

Then they were coming at him, leaping from the open door, hundreds of them, it seemed, faintly seen in the light of the flash that lay upon the ground—horrible little monsters such as one would never see except in some sweating dream. He reversed the gun, scarcely realizing that he did it, grasping the barrels in both his hands, using it as a club, flailing with it blindly as they came swarming out at him.

Jaws fastened on an ankle and a heavy body struck him in the chest. Claws raked his left leg from hip to knee and he knew that he was going down and that once he was down they would finish him.

He sagged to his knees and now one of them had him by the arm and he tried to fight it off, while another clawed his back to ribbons. He tipped over on one side and ducked down his head, covering it with his one free arm, drawing up his knees to protect his belly.

And that was all. They no longer chewed or ripped him. He jerked up his head and saw them, flitting shadows, moving out into the dark. The beam of the fallen flashlight caught one of them momentarily and for the first time he really saw the sort of creatures that had been in the henhouse and at the sight of it he bawled in utter terror.

Then it was gone—all of them were gone—and he was alone in the yard. He tried to get up. Halfway erect, his legs folded under him and he fell heavily. He crawled toward the house, clawing at the ground to pull himself along. There was a wetness on one arm and one leg, and a stinging pain was beginning in his back.

The kitchen window glowed with a lighted lamp. Tige came out from beneath the porch and crawled toward him, belly flat against the ground, whining. Mary, in her nightgown, was running down the stairs.

"Get the sheriff," he yelled at her, gasping with the effort. "Phone the sheriff!"

She raced across the yard and knelt beside him, trying to get her hands beneath his body to lift him.

He pushed her away. "Get the sheriff! The sheriff has to know."

"But you're hurt. You're bleeding."

"I'm all right," he told her fiercely. "They're gone. But the others must be warned. You didn't see them. You don't know."

"I have to get you in. Call the doctor."

"The sheriff first," he said. "Then the doctor."

She rose and raced back to the house. He tried to crawl, covered a few feet, and then lay still. Tige came crawling out to meet him, edged in close to him, began to lick his face.

30

ONCE the men were seated around the table in the conference room, Dr. Samuel Ives opened the discussion.

"This meeting," he said, "despite the solemnity of the occasion which brings us together in the dead of night, marks what for all of us of the present must be an exciting event. All of our professional lives most of us have at times puzzled over the fundamental nature of time irreversibility. A couple of us, myself and Dr. Asbury Brooks, have spent a great deal of time in its study. I am of the opinion that Dr. Brooks will not take it badly if I say we have made little, if any, progress in our studies of this fundamental question. While the lay person may question the validity of such study, viewing time as a philosophical rather than a physical concept, the fact remains that the physical laws with which all of us work are embedded in this somewhat mysterious thing that we call time. We must ask ourselves, if we are to completely understand the concepts that we employ, both in our daily lives and our continuing investigations into many areas of science, what may be the physical interrelationships underlying the expansion of the universe, information theory, and the thermodynamic, electromagnetic, biological and statistical arrows of time. In the description of any physical phenomenon, the time variable is a parameter, at the most elementary level. We have wondered if there were such a thing as universal time or whether it may be only a feature of boundary conditions. There are some of us who think that the latter may be the true explanation, that in the universe the time factor was perhaps rather randomly set at the moment of the beginning of the universe and has persisted ever since. And all of us, I think, are aware that our thinking about time must be overwhelmingly prejudiced by our intuitive notions about the direction of time flow and that this may be one of the factors which has made it so difficult for us to understand and formulate any real theories about this thing that we call time.''

He looked across the table at the three men from the future. ''I must beg your indulgence for this sort of introduction to our discussion, remarks that, in view of what you have learned, may sound somewhat silly. But I did think it important to set out our own views and study into some sort of perspective. But now that I have said this much, I think that it is your turn to talk and I assure you that all of us will listen most attentively. Which one of you would like to begin?''

Hardwicke and Cummings looked at each other questioningly. Finally Hardwicke said, ''Perhaps I might as well. I must express the deep appreciation all three of us feel for your willingness to meet with us at this unusual hour. And I am afraid that we are about to disappoint you, for I must tell you that we know very little more about the fundamental nature of time than you do. We have asked ourselves some of the same questions you have asked and have found no real answers. . . .''

''But you can travel in time,'' said Brooks. ''That would argue that you must know something of it. You must have at least a basic understanding. . . .''

''What we found,'' said Hardwicke, ''is that we are not the only universe. There are at least two universes coexisting within the same space, but universes so fundamentally different from one another that neither would be ordinarily aware of the other. At the moment I will not go into the manner in which this other universe was detected or what we know of it. It is not, however, a contraterrene universe, so there is, so far as we know, no danger from it. I might add that the first hint of its existence came from a study of the strangeness of certain particles. Not that the particles themselves are a part of this other universe, but because, in certain instances, they can react to certain not-entirely-understood conditions in the other universe. Two totally different universes. The other made up of particles and interactions which have little to do with the particles and in-

116

teractions of our universe, although, as I have indicated, there can be interactions, but on so small a scale that only blind, dumb luck could bring them to one's notice. Fortunately, researchers experienced that blind luck. And it was mostly luck, too, that revealed to us something else about the second universe. I often wonder if luck, for want of a better word, might not be a factor that should be in itself the subject of a study with a view to a better determination of its parameters. As I say, we found out one thing else about the other universe, a very simple thing and yet, when one thinks about it, a rather devastating concept. What we found was that the arrow of time in the second universe was flowing in exactly the opposite direction to the one it traveled in our universe. While undoubtedly in that universe it was moving from the universe's past toward its future, in relation to this universe, it was traveling from our future toward our past.''

"There is one thing that puzzles me," said Ives. "You were dealing with a very complex matter and yet in twenty years or so. . . ."

"It is not as remarkable as you think," said Cummings. "There was a crash project, certainly, to achieve time travel, but before the project was begun we were in possession of the knowledge that Dr. Hardwicke has outlined. On your old time track the fact of the second universe was discovered somewhat less than a hundred years from now. It had been investigated for almost four centuries before we finally put the time arrow of the second universe to work. As a matter of fact, much significant work had been done on the possibility of using the opposite time direction of the second universe as a time travel medium. All we had to do was give the investigation a final push. I think the method might have been worked out earlier, even before the invasion by the aliens, if there had been any reason for it. But, aside from scientific curiosity, there wasn't. Under ordinary circumstances, there's not much attraction to time travel if you can move in only the one direction and there's no possibility of returning.''

"Once we decided," said Hardwicke, "that the only way in which we could survive was to travel backwards into time, much of the real work already had been done. In all the history of scientific inquiry there always has been a certain segment of the population that questions the validity of pure research. What

117

is the good of it, they ask. How is it going to help us? What can we use it for? I think that our situation is a perfect example of the value of basic research. The work that had been done on the second universe and its opposite-direction time flow had been pure research, the spending of effort and funds on something that seemed to offer no chance at all of any benefit or return. And yet, as things turned out, it did have a return. It offered the human race a chance to save itself."

"As I understand it," said Brooks, "what you have done is to make use of the opposite time flow of the other universe to bring you here. Somehow or other your time tunnels trap the opposite flow. You step into the opposite flow in your own present time and step out of it at our present time. But to do this you must manage to speed up the time flow tremendously and must be able to control it."

"That," said Hardwicke, "was the hard part of the job. Not the theory of it, for the theory had been worked out, but the implementation of the theory. As it turned out, it was unbelievably simple, although on the face of it complex."

"You think it is in the range of our present technology?"

"We are sure of it," said Hardwicke. "That is why we chose this particular time. We had to select a time target that held men who would understand and accept the theory and other men, engineers, who could build the necessary equipment. There were other factors, as well, that we took into consideration. We needed to reach a time where the intellectual and moral climate was such that there would be a willingness to provide us the help we needed. We also had to find time where the productivity of the economy was such that it could supply us with the implements and tools we would need to start life over in the Miocene. Perhaps we are being unfair to hope for so much from you. We have one justification. If we had not come back, to this time bracket or some other, the race of man would have ended some five hundred years from now. As it is, you have been shifted to a new time track, a phenomenon we can take the time later to discuss, if you should wish, and there now is a chance, although no certainty, that you can continue into the future with no alien invasion."

"Dr. Osborne," said Ives, "has so far taken no part in this discussion. Is there something you might like to add?"

Osborne shook his head. "All of this is beyond my competence, gentlemen. I'm not a physicist, but a geologist, with leanings toward paleontology. I'm simply along for the ride. Later, if some of you might want to discuss the Miocene, which is our eventual destination, that is something I could talk about."

"I, for one," said Brooks, "would be interested in hearing you right now. I have heard there is some proposal that the present population of the Earth go back into the Miocene with you. This is something, I would imagine, that might appeal to some of the more venturesome among us. There is always a feeling in many people that they have lost something by being born after the age of geographic pioneering. There would be a strong appeal to the idea of going back to a time where many of the present-day restrictions might be shed. I wonder if you would be willing to tell us something of what we might expect to find in the Miocene."

"If you feel it is appropriate," said Osborne, "I would be glad to. You must understand, of course, that we are dealing in some suppositions, although we can be fairly sure of certain facts. The main reason we picked the Miocene is that this was the time when grass first appeared upon the Earth. There are reasons we believe this, although I won't go into them right now. For one thing, it is the time when true grazing animals acquired a kind of teeth adapted for grass eating. Grazing animals, in the early part of the epoch, seem to have increased rapidly. The climate became somewhat more arid, although by our calculations there still would be plenty of rainfall for agriculture. Many of the huge forest tracts gave way to grassy plains, supporting huge herds of herbivores. We know something of these herbivores, although I think it may be possible there may have been many species of which we have no paleontological evidence.

"There would be great herds of oreodonts, sheep-sized animals that may have been remote relatives of the camels. There would be camels, too, although far smaller than the ones we know today. We could expect to find small horses, the size of ponies. There might be a number of rhinos. Sometime during the Miocene, probably in its early days, elephants migrated to North America over the Bering land bridge. They'd be fourtuskers, smaller than today's elephants. One of the more dangerous animals would be the giant pig, big as an oxen and with skulls that measure four feet long. They could be ugly customers to meet. With so many herbivores running in herds on the prairies, the Miocene could be expected to have its full quota of carnivores, both canines and cats. Probably you'd find the old ancestors of the sabretooths. That's only a quick rundown. There is much more. The point is that we believe the Miocene was a time of rather rapid evolutionary development, with the fauna expanding into new genera and species, characterized, perhaps, by a tendency for animals to increase in size. There might be a number of holdovers from the Oligocene, even from the Eocene. I suppose some of the mammals might be dangerous. There could be poisonous snakes and insects—I'm not entirely sure of that. As a matter of fact, we have little evidence along those lines.''

''In your estimation, however,'' said Brooks, ''it would be livable. Man could get along.''

''We are sure he can,'' said Osborne. ''The great forests of past ages would be giving way to prairies, and while there still would remain plenty of wood for man's use, there would be great open spaces waiting for the plow. There would be grass to support man's livestock. The heavy rainfall that characterized some of the earlier epochs would have decreased. Until he got started, man could live off the land. There would be plenty of game, nuts, berries, fruit, roots. Fishing should be good. We're not as certain about the climate as we'd like to be, but there is some evidence that it would be more equable than now. The summers probably would be as warm, the winters not so cold. You understand this can't be guaranteed.''

''I understand that,'' said Brooks, ''but in any case, you are set on going.''

''We have,'' said Osborne, ''very little choice.''

31

STEVE WILSON came back into the pressroom. The desk lamp still was lit, painting a circle of light in the darkened room. The teletypes muttered against the wall. Almost three o'clock, he thought. He'd have to get some sleep. Even with the best of luck, even if he could go to sleep, he had at the most four hours or so before he'd have to be back on the job again.

As he approached the desk, Alice Gale rose from the chair where she had been sitting in the dark. She still wore the white robe. He wondered if it was all she had. Perhaps it was, he told himself, for the people from the future had carried little luggage with them.

"Mr. Wilson," she said, "we have been waiting for you, hoping that you would return. My father wants to talk with you."

"Certainly," said Wilson. "Good morning, Mr. Gale."

Gale came out of the darkness and laid his attaché case upon the desk top.

"I am somewhat embarrassed," he said, "I find myself in a position that could be awkward. I wonder if you would listen to me and tell me how to go about this thing I want to do. You appear to be a man who knows his way around."

Wilson, moving to the desk, stiffened. The whole thing, he sensed, as Gale had said, had an awkwardness about it. He sensed he was going to be placed in a difficult position. He waited.

"We are well aware," said Gale, "that our coming from the future has placed a terrible burden upon the governments and the peoples of the world. We did the little that we could. In areas where we knew there would be food shortages, we arranged the delivery of wheat and other foodstuffs. We stand ready to supply any labor that will be required, for we represent a large, and idle, labor force. But the building of the tunnels and the supplying to us of the tools we will need in the Miocene will represent a vast expenditure of funds. . . ."

He reached down into the circle of light on the desk top and, unlatching the case, opened it. It was packed with small leather bags. Lifting one of these, he pulled it open and poured out on the desk top a shower of cut stones that flashed and glittered in the light.

"Diamonds," he said.

Wilson gulped. "But why?" he whispered. "Why diamonds? Why bring them to me?"

"It was the only way," said Gale, "that we could bring anything of value in small enough volume to be conveniently transported. And we know that, if dumped upon the market all at once, these stones would ruin prices. But if they were fed into the market, a few at a time, surreptitiously, they would have but small effect. This especially would be true if their existence were kept secret. And we have been very careful that there be no duplications, that there are no paradoxes. It would have been possible to have brought from the future many of the famous gems that now exist and are well known. We have not done this. All the stones in this case are ones which were found and cut in your future. None of them is known at the present day."

"Put them back," said Wilson, horrified. "Good God, man, can you imagine what might happen if it became known what was in that case. Billions of dollars. . . ."

"Yes, many billions," Gale said calmly. "At the going prices in this age, perhaps as much as a trillion. Worth much more than they were in our time. We, five hundred years from now, did not place as great a value on such things as you do now."

Unhurriedly he picked up the stones, put them back into the bag, fitted the bag back into the case, closed and latched it.

"I wish most heartily," said Wilson, "that you had not told me of this."

"But we had to," Alice said. "Don't you see? You are the

only one we know, the only one that we can trust. We could safely tell you and you could tell us what to do.''

Wilson struggled to put some calmness into his words. "Let us all sit down," he said, "and talk this over. Let's not speak too loudly. I don't think there is anyone around, but someone could walk in on us."

They went back beyond the circle of light, pulled three chairs together and sat down.

"Now suppose you tell me," Wilson said, "what this is all about.''

"We had thought," said Gale, "that the proceeds from these stones, wisely marketed, could compensate in part some of the actual costs that helping us entails. Not one government, not one people, but all the governments and all the peoples of the Earth. Putting the proceeds into a fund, perhaps, and once all the stones are sold, allocating the monies in proportion to the actual costs involved.''

"In that case. . . ."

"I anticipate your question. Why were the stones not divided and offered each government involved? There are two reasons this was not done. The more people who are involved, the greater the possibility that the news would leak out. Our only chance was to keep the number who knew of it at a minimum. Among us there are not more than six who know. Here, you are the only one so far. There is, as well, the matter of trust. On the basis of history, we knew there were few governments we could trust—actually, only two, you and the British. On the basis of our study, we decided on the United States. There had been some feeling the United Nations should be the organization entrusted with the gems. But, quite frankly, we had little confidence in the UN. I was supposed to hand the stones to the President. I decided against this when I realized how many problems he had weighing on his mind, how he was forced to depend upon the judgment of so many people.''

"I know only one thing," said Wilson. "You can't keep on carrying this case around with you. You have to be placed under security until it has been put into some safe place. Fort Knox, probably, if the government is willing to accept it.''

"You mean, Mr. Wilson, that I'll have to be placed under guard. I'm not sure I like that.''

"Christ, I don't know," said Wilson. "I don't even know where to begin."

He reached for the phone and dialed. "Jane, you still on duty? Do you know—has the President retired?"

"An hour ago," said Jane.

"Good," said Wilson. "He should have long before then."

"Is it important, Steve? He left orders if there was anything important that he should be called."

"No, this can wait. Do you think you can get hold of Jerry Black?"

"I'll try. I think he's still around."

The room was silent except for the teletypes. Gale and Alice sat unstirring in their chairs. Light still shone beneath the press lounge doors, but there was no sound of typing.

"We're sorry to upset you so," Alice said to Wilson. "But we were at out wits' ends. We didn't know what to do."

"It's all right," said Wilson.

"You don't know how much this means to us," she said. "The rest of the people may not know till later, but we'll know. That we did not come as beggars. That we paid our way. That's important to us."

Footsteps came down the corridor and turned in at the door.

"What's going on, Steve?" asked Jerry Black.

"We need a couple of men," said Wilson.

"I'm one of them," said Black. "I can find another."

"It'll be a favor," said Wilson. "I have no jurisdiction. I'm acting on my own. It'll be until tomorrow morning, as soon as I can see the President."

"It's OK," said Black, "if it's for the President."

"I think," said Wilson, "that it might be for him."

"All right," said Black. "What is it?"

"Mr. Gale has an attaché case. I won't tell you what is in it. You wouldn't want to know. But it's important. And I want him to keep it—him and no one else. Until we know what to do with it."

"That can be managed. You think it needs two of us?"

"I'd feel better if there were two of you."

"No trouble," said Black. "Let me use your phone."

32

DAWN was graying in the eastern sky when Enoch Raven sat down to his typewriter. Outside the window lay the green Virginia hills, and in the trees and shrubs a few awakening birds began their twittering and chirping.

He flexed his fingers over the keyboard and then began to type, writing steadily, without pause for thought. He had made it a rule, these many years, to have it all thought out before he sat down to write, to have run the subject matter through his mind, refining it and sharpening it so that the readers of his column need never search for meaning. The meaning must be there for all to see, the logic well developed.

He wrote:

The world today faces what may be its greatest crisis and the strangeness of this lies in the fact that the crisis comes not by the ordinary channels we have come to associate with crisis. Although, when one thinks it through, it becomes apparent that it does parallel a crisis situation we long have recognized—overpopulation and the economic problems which could spring from it. As short a time ago as last Sunday morning, however, no one in his right mind could remotely have imagined that the over-population which had been feared and preached against so long, could have come upon us overnight.

Now that it has, we are faced with a situation that must be solved, not over a long period of careful planning, but in a matter, perhaps, of weeks. The brutal fact of the matter is that we can feed the hordes of people who have come to us for help over only a very limited span of time. They, themselves, are frank in admitting that they were aware of the problems their coming would create and in consequence of this have brought us the knowledge and the tools we will need in solving them. All that remains is that we use these tools forthwith. For this to be done requires the willing cooperation of every one of us. This phrase is not used lightly, nor in its hortatory political sense, but in a very personal way. Every one of us, each of us, all of us.

What is needed from the most of us is forbearance, a willingness to bear certain sacrifices, to tolerate certain inconveniences. It may mean that there will be less food, and not so good, for us to eat. We may have to wait for delivery of that new car. We may not be able to buy a new lawn mower when the old one that is now on its last legs finally breaks down. The economic energy and direction that under normal circumstances would be channeled into the production and distribution of items and services we need must be cancelled not only into sending our far descendants back deeper into time, but into providing them with the equipment, tools and supplies they will need to build a viable culture. It may be that Detroit may be called upon to turn out plows and other implements rather than cars. It may be that, voluntarily, or by government decree, we may have to ration ourselves. Wise as the actions taken by President Henderson may have been in calling for a bank and transactions holiday and a price and wage freeze, a case can be made that he should have taken one further step by issuing a strong warning against hoarding. While we can ill afford to deal in a bureaucratic manner with the press of events that have been forced upon us, it would seem that some move toward a strict rationing of food and other items vital to the continuing economy should be taken at once. It is quite understandable, for political reasons, why Mr. Henderson might have been reluctant to do this. But it is upon such unpopular actions, or the failure to take these actions, that we will stand or fall.

It would seem scarcely necessary to point out that such actions as the President has taken should be taken by other nations as well. It is reliably understood that Britain, Russia, France, Germany, Japan, China, and possibly other nations may have already taken corresponding actions before these words see the light of print. But the action must be worldwide rather than the actions of just a few of the more powerful nations. The problem that we face is a worldwide problem and for it to be solved temporary economic strictures must be imposed not only upon the larger economic units, but upon the entire world.

The appearance of the people from the future undoubtedly will call forth from the various intellectual factions a wide variety of opinions, many of which undoubtedly will be ill-founded. This is well illustrated by the public agony which is being exhibited by the Rev. Jake Billings, one of the more colorful of our evangelists, over the revelation that the people of five hundred years from now have forsaken religion as a rather footless factor in the lives of mankind. Distressing as this may be to the professional religionists, it is scarcely a consideration which has any bearing upon the matter now immediately at hand. Not only on this point, but on many other points, profound questions will be raised, but now is not the time to expend any noticeable amount of energy in trying to answer or resolve them. They will do no more than to further divide a population which, under the best of circumstances, is bound to be divided by the basic task which has been brought upon us.

We have not as yet had the time, nor indeed the facts, to enable us at this moment to form a true evaluation of the situation. While we have been made aware of some of the basic facts, there may be other facts that are as yet unknown, or perhaps some which, in the press of other considerations, have not become apparent. It may well be that some of the emphasis may be at fault—not as a result of someone trying to obscure the importance of any fact, but simply because there has not been the opportunity to assess the various factors and give each the weight of importance which rightly belongs to it.

There is no time, of course, for deliberate consideration of the crisis; in essence, the world must act with more expediency than may be entirely wise. The very fact that expediency is necessary calls for a public forbearance that is usually not desirable when great issues are at stake. A storm of criticism and a violent putting forward of opinions at variance with official opinion and action will accomplish nothing other than an impedance to a solution which must come quickly if it is to come at all. The men in Washington, at Whitehall and in the Kremlin may be wrong on many points, but their various publics must realize that they are acting not out of the perversity of stupidity, but in honest good faith, doing what they consider proper to be done.

Insofar as the republics of the world are concerned, this is not the way things should be done. Democracy demands, and rightly, that all men should have a voice in their government and in governmental decisions and actions, that all viewpoints be given full consideration, that there be no arbitrary decisions counter to the public will. But today we cannot afford the luxury of such an idealistic concept. The situation may not be handled as many of us would wish that it would be handled, some toes undoubtedly will be trod upon, certain ideas of justice and propriety may be outraged. But to accept all of this, if not in silence, at least without raising too great an outcry, is a part of that forbearance that is called for.

This is not one country that is threatened, not one political party nor one political fortune, not one people nor one region, but the entire world. This commentator has no way of knowing what will happen. I cannot even guess. I am aware that there may be much that I will not like, much that I will consider might have been done differently or better. In the past there has been no hesitancy on my part to place personal opinion upon record and at a later date, after this is over, I suppose I might not be above the pointing out of glaring errors as I may have perceived them. But from this day forward I shall, as a personal contribution to the forbearance which appears to me so necessary, exercise stern censorship upon, if not my thoughts, at least upon my typewriter. I am hereby enrolling myself as charter member in the Keep Your Mouth Shut, Enoch Club. The membership is wide open and I invite all of you to join.

33

HE had somehow climbed a tree and got out on a limb and had been hanging onto it, for no reason that seemed quite logical, when a sudden violent wind had come up and now he was hanging grimly to the branch which was whipping in the wind. He knew that at any moment his grasp might be torn loose and he'd be thrown to the ground. But when he looked down, he saw, with horror, that there wasn't any ground.

From somewhere far off a voice was speaking to him, but he was so intent on maintaining his grip upon the branch that he was unable to distinguish the words. The shaking became even more violent. "Steve," the voice was saying. "Steve, wake up." His eyes came open a slit and he realized that he was in no tree. A distorted face swam crazily just above him. No one had such a face.

"Wake up, Steve," said a voice that was Henry Hunt's. "The President is asking for you." Wilson lifted a fist and scrubbed his eyes. The face, no longer distorted, was the face of Henry Hunt.

The face receded into the distance as the *Times* man straightened up. Wilson swung his feet off the couch, sat up. Sunlight was streaming through the windows of the press lounge.

"What time is it?" he asked.

"Almost eight."

Wilson squinted up at Hunt. "You get any sleep?" he asked.

"I went home for a couple of hours. I couldn't sleep. Things kept spinning in my head. So I came back." He picked a jacket off the floor. "This yours?" he asked.

Wilson nodded groggily. "I got to get washed up," he said. "I got to comb my hair."

He rose to his feet, took the jacket from Hunt and tucked it underneath his arm. "What's going on?" he asked.

"What you might expect," said Hunt. "The wires are clogged with screams of anguish over the business holiday. How come you didn't tip us off, Steve?"

"I didn't know. He never said a word about it."

"Well, that's all right," said Hunt. "We should have guessed it. Can you imagine what would have happened if the exchanges were open?"

"Any word about the monster? '

"Rumor. Nothing solid. One rumor says another got through in Africa. Somewhere in the Congo. Christ, they'll never find it there."

"The Congo's not all jungle, Henry."

"Where it's supposed to have happened, it is."

Wilson headed for the washroom. When he returned, Hunt had a cup of coffee for him.

"Thanks," he said. He sipped the hot brew and shuddered. "I don't know if I can face the day," he said. "Any idea of what the President has in mind?"

Hunt shook his head.

"Judy in yet?"

"Not yet, Steve."

Wilson put the cup, still half full, down on the coffee table. "Thanks for getting me up and going," he said. "I'll see you later."

He went through the door into the pressroom. The lamp he had forgotten to turn off still shone feebly down upon the desk. In the corridor outside footsteps went smartly up and down. He straightened his jacket and went out.

Two men were with the President. One was General Daniel Foote, the other was one of the refugees, rigged out in a mountain-man outfit.

"Good morning, Mr. President," said Wilson.

"Good morning, Steve. You get any sleep?"

"An hour or so."

"You know General Foote, of course," said the President. "The gentleman with him is Isaac Wolfe. Dr. Wolfe is a biologist. He brings us rather frightening news. I thought that you should hear it."

Wolfe was a heavy man—heavy of body, deep in the chest, standing on short, solid legs. His head, covered by a rat-nest of graying hair, seemed oversize.

He stepped quickly forward and shook Wilson's hand. "I am sorry," he said, "to be the bearer of such disturbing facts."

"Last night," said the President, "rather sometime this morning, a farmer not far from Harper's Ferry was wakened by something in his chicken coop. He went out and found the henhouse full of strange beasts, the size, perhaps, of half-grown hogs. He fired at them and they got away, all except one which the shotgun blast almost cut in two. The farmer was attacked. He's in the hospital. He'll live, I'm told, but he was fairly well chewed up. From what he says there can be little doubt the things in the henhouse were a new batch of the monsters."

"But that's impossible," said Wilson. "The monster escaped only a few. . . ."

"Dr. Wolfe came to me last evening," said Foote, "shortly after the monster escaped from the tunnel. I frankly didn't believe what he told me, but when the report of the henhouse episode came in from an officer of a search party out in West Virginia, I looked him up and asked him to come to the White House. I'm sorry, Doctor, for not believing you to start with."

"But it's still impossible," said Wilson.

"No, no," said Wolfe. "It is not impossible. We are dealing here with an organism entirely different from anything you've ever known. The evolutionary processes of these monsters are like nothing you have ever guessed. Their reaction to environmental stress is beyond all belief. We had known something of it and had deduced the rest, but I am convinced that under stresses such as the escaped monster is experiencing, the developmental procedures can be speeded up to a fantastic rate. An hour or so to hatch, an hour later hunting food. The same pressure that is placed upon the parent is transmitted to the young. For both the parent and the young this is a crisis situation. The parent is aware of this, of course; the young, of course, would not be. But in some strange manner which I can't pretend to know, a sense of desperate urgency is transmitted to the egg. Hatch swiftly, grow up quickly, scatter widely, reach the egg-laying stage as soon as possible. It is a genetic reaction to a survival threat. The young monsters would be driven by an evolutionary force that in an earthly life form would be inconceivable. They are members of a strange race that has a unique, an inborn, capability to use every trick in the evolutionary pattern to its advantage."

Wilson found a chair and sat down limply. He looked at the President. "Has any of this leaked out?"

"No," said the President, "it has not. The farmer's wife phoned the sheriff. The military search party had just reached the area and was talking with the sheriff when the call came in. The officer in charge clamped on a security lid. That is why you're here, Steve. We can't keep this buttoned up. It'll leak out—if not this particular incident, then others. There may be hundreds of these tiny monsters out there in the mountains. They'll be seen and reported. The reports will begin to pile up. We can't sit on all of them, nor should we."

"The problem," said Wilson, "is how to release the news without scaring the pants off everybody."

"If we don't tell them," said the President, "we create a credibility gap that will make everything we do suspect. And there is, as well, the matter of public safety."

"In a few days," said Foote, "all the mountains will be full of full-grown monsters. They probably will scatter. We can hunt some of them down, but not all of them. Probably only a small percentage of them. The only way we can manage it is to put in every man we can lay our hands on to hunt them down."

"They will scatter, that is right," said Wolfe. "By scattering, they will insure their chances of survival. And they can travel fast. By another day, perhaps, they'll be up in New England, down into Georgia. They will keep, at first, to the mountainous terrain because it would give them the best concealment. In time they'll begin branching out from the mountains."

"How long would you guess," asked Wilson, "before they begin laying eggs?"

Wolfe spread his hands. "Who can know?" he said.

"Your best guess."

"A week. Two weeks. I do not know."

"How many eggs in a clutch?"

"A couple of dozen. You must understand we do not know. We found only a few nests."

"When will they begin their killing?"

"Now. Right now. They must eat to grow. They must do a lot of killing. Wild animals, farm animals, occasionally humans. Not many humans to start with. By killing men they draw attention to themselves. Warlike as they may be, they still will know they are vulnerable because there are so few of them. They may be psychopathic killers, but they aren't stupid."

"We have some troops out now," said the President. "We'll have to use many more. Get planes and helicopters up to spot the monsters. I talked to Sandburg just a while ago. He is coming in. He'll know what we can do. This means we call out the reserves, perhaps call back some troops from abroad. Not only do we have to hunt the monsters, but we have to maintain the camps for the refugees."

"We do not wish to stand idly by," said Wolfe. "There are many thousands of us. Give us arms and we'll go in side by side with your military. We know about these creatures and we were the ones who brought them here. We have a duty and. . . ."

"Later," said the President, "there'll be plenty you can do. Getting you into the field would be a tremendous task. Right at the moment we must depend upon our own men."

"How about the people out there in the mountains?" asked Wilson. "Do we pull them out?"

The President shook his head. "I don't think so, Steve. We have, right now, all the refugees we can handle. And I'm inclined to think that at the moment our monsters may not be too aggressive. They're probably concentrating on staying out of sight. There may be some incidents, but we must be prepared to accept those. It's all that we can do."

"I think, sir, that you are right," said Wolfe. "They are outnumbered now and must build up their strength. In any event, the young aliens will not, for a time, be too great a menace. They'll have to put on some size and weight. I suppose that, as well, they may know that they face more deadly weapons, in much greater numbers, than we could ever bring against them. We had lived in peace so long we had lost most of the military techniques and we started from scratch in weapon building.''

"You face a busy day, Mr. President," said Foote. "If there is nothing further that you wish from us. . . .''

The President rose and came around the desk. He shook both by the hand. "Thanks for coming by," he said. "This is something we must get busy on immediately.''

Wilson rose to leave. "Do I call in the press immediately?" he asked. "Or should I wait until after you have talked with Defense?''

The President hesitated, considering. "I should think right away," he said. "I'd like for us to be the first to tell them. The military has the lid clamped down, but it won't stay clamped for long. Some of the people from the Hill are coming in to see me. It would be better if they knew about this before they arrived.''

"There's another matter," said Wilson. "You were asleep and I didn't want to wake you. There's a dispatch case full of diamonds. . . .''

"Diamonds? What have diamonds got to do with this?''

"It's a rather awkward business, sir," said Wilson. "You recall that case Gale was carrying. . . .''

"There were diamonds in that case?''

"It was packed with sacks. He opened one sack and poured out diamonds on the desk. He told me the rest of the sacks also contained diamonds and I'm inclined to believe him. The refugees had the idea they could turn them over to us to pay whatever was laid out to send them back to the Miocene.''

"I would like to have seen your face," said the President, "when he poured out the diamonds. What, may I ask, did you do about it?''

"I called in Jerry Black and put Gale under guard. I insisted that he keep the diamonds.''

"I guess," said the President, "that was all that you could do. I think maybe I should call in the Treasury to take temporary custody and check with Reilly Douglas about the legality of it all. Did you get any idea how much the diamonds might be worth?''

"Gale said, at present prices, perhaps a trillion dollars. That is, if they can be fed into the market slowly, without depressing prices. They're not, you understand, for us alone, but for the entire world. Gale wants to leave them with us, in trust for all the governments. He said we were the only government they felt that they could trust.''

''You realize, of course, how sticky this could be? If word of this leaked out. . . .''

''To be entirely fair,'' said Wilson, ''we still must realize that they are only trying to be helpful. They want to pay their way.''

''Yes, I know,'' said the President. ''We'll have to see what Reilly says about it.''

34

SINCE early morning the crowd had been gathering in Lafayette Park across the avenue from the White House. It was still the quiet and watchful group that had stood the Sunday vigil, with its stolid watchfulness. But now there were a few placards and there had been none before. One of the placards, crudely lettered, read BACK TO THE MIOCENE. Another read BRING ON YOUR SABERTOOTHS. Still another: LET US LEAVE THIS LOUSY WORLD.

A newsman pushed his way through the crowd, zeroing in on the whiskered youth who bore the BACK TO THE MIOCENE placard.

"Would you mind telling me," he asked, "what is going on?"

"Man," said the youth impatiently, "it is there for you to read. It says it loud and clear."

"It puzzles me," said the newsman, "what you are trying to prove. Or don't you have a point to make?"

"No points this time," the sign carrier told him. "In the past we have tried to prove some points and have mostly gotten nowhere." He made a thumb in the direction of the White House. "The man don't listen too good. No one listens too good."

"This time," said a girl who stood beside the sign carrier, "we're not proving anything at all. We're simply saying what we want to do and that's go back to the Miocene."

"Or the Eocene," said another girl. "Or the Paleocene. Just anywhere at all to get away from this scruffy place. We want to leave this crummy world and get another start. We want to go back and build the kind of world we want. We've been trying for years to change this society and we've gotten just exactly nowhere. And when we saw we couldn't change it, we tried to get out of it. That's what the communes are all about. But the society won't let us go. It reaches out and hauls us back. It will not let us go."

"Finally," said the sign carrier, "here's a way to get shut of it. If these people from the future can travel to the past, there's no reason why we shouldn't. There aren't many people who would be sorry to see us go. Most of them would be glad to see us go."

"I suppose," said the newsman, "that this could be called a movement. Most of the other things you people have done have been labeled movements. Would you mind telling me how many of you. . . ."

"Not at all," said the first girl. "Not more than fifteen or twenty of us now. But you write your story and let us get a news spot on television and there'll be thousands of us. They'll be coming from Chicago and New York, from Boston and Los Angeles. There'll be more of us than this town can hold. Because, you see, this is the first real chance we've had to get away."

"That's all right," the newsman said. "I can see your point. But how do you go about it? Storm across the street and pound on the White House door?"

"If you mean," said the sign carrier, "that no one will pay attention to us, you may be right. But twenty-four hours from now they'll pay attention to us. Forty-eight hours from now they'll be out here in the street talking with us."

"But you realize, of course, there are no time tunnels yet. There may never be. It will take materials and manpower. . . ."

"They got their manpower right here, mister. All anyone has to do is ask. Hand us picks and shovels. Hand us wrenches. Hand us anything at all and tell us what to do. We'll work until we drop. We'll do anything to get away from here. We don't want any pay for working; we don't want anything at all except to be allowed to go."

"You tell them that," said the second girl. "You put it just the way we say."

"We're not out to kick up any trouble," said the sign carrier. "We don't want to cause any fuss. We just want to let them know. This is the only way we can."

"We won't ask anything if they'll only let us leave," said the first girl. "We would like some hoes and axes, maybe some pots and pans. But if they won't give us anything, we'll go empty-handed."

"Prehistoric men made out with stone," said the sign carrier. "If we have to, we can do the same."

"Why stand there listening to them?" asked a burly individual with a cigar stuck in his mouth. "Hell, all they do is talk. They all are full of crap. They don't want to go anywhere. They just want to stir up trouble."

"You're wrong," said the man with the sign. "We mean exactly what we say. What makes you think we want to stay here, along with jerks like you?"

The man with the cigar made a grab at the sign and one of the girls kicked him in the shin. Wincing from the kick, his reaching fingers missed the sign. The carrier clunked him on the head with it. A man who had been standing beside the man with the cigar hit the sign carrier on the jaw.

A scuffle exploded and the police came in and broke it up.

35

JUDY was at her desk. Notes were beginning to accumulate on the spindle. The lights on the console were blinking.

"You get any sleep?" asked Wilson.

She looked up at him. "A little. I lay awake thinking, scared. It's not good, is it, Steve?"

"Not good," he said. "It's too big for us to handle. If it weren't for the time element, it wouldn't be so bad. If we only had a little time."

She gestured toward the door leading to the lounge. "You won't tell them that, will you?"

He grinned. "No, I won't tell them that."

"They've been asking when you're going to see them."

"Fairly soon," he said.

"I might as well tell you," she said. "No use waiting. I am going home. Back to Ohio."

"But I need you here."

"You can get a girl from the secretarial pool. Couple of days and you won't know the difference."

"That's not what I mean. . . ."

"I know what you mean. You need me to shack up with. It's been like that for how long—six months? It's this damn town. It makes everything dirty that it touches. Somewhere else it might have worked for us. But it isn't working here."

"Damn it, Judy," he said, "what's got into you? Because I didn't come out last night. . . ."

"Partly that, perhaps. Not all that, of course. I know why you had to stay. But it was so lonely and so many things had happened and I sat there thinking and got scared. I tried to call my mother and the lines were busy. A poor scared girl, for Christ's sake, running back to Mama. But suddenly everything was different. I wasn't a sleek, competent Washington hussy any longer; I was a kid in pigtails in a little town deep in Ohio. It all started with my getting scared. Tell me honest now, I had a right to be scared."

"You had a right," he said soberly. "I'm half scared myself. Everyone is scared."

"What's going to happen to us?"

"Damned if I know. But that wasn't what we were talking about."

"Monsters running loose," she said. "Too many mouths to feed. Everyone fighting one another or getting set to fight."

"We were talking about you going to Ohio. I'm not going to ask you do you really mean it, because I know you do. I suppose that you are lucky to have a place to run to. Most of us have no place. I'd like to ask you to stay, but that would be unfair. What's more, it would be selfish. But I still wish you would."

"I have a plane reservation," she said. "With the phone tied up and all, I was surprised to get one. The country's in a panic. In a time like this you get that terribly helpless feeling."

"You won't like Ohio. Once you get there, you won't like it. If you're scared in Washington, you'll be scared in Ohio."

"I still am going, Steve. Come six-fifteen tonight and I'll be on that plane."

"There's nothing I can say?"

"There's nothing you can say," she said.

"Then you'd better let the press in. I have some news for them."

36

SENATOR ANDREW OAKES hitched himself up slightly from the depths of the chair in which he'd sank. "I'm not right sure, Mr. President," he said, "that it's wise to bring home all the troops. We need to keep our bases manned. And it seems to me we're allowing ourselves to get flustered just a mite too soon. Some itty bitty monsters raid a chicken coop out in West Virginia and we start bringing home the troops. It don't seem scarcely right. And I'm not sure it was too smart, either, to tell the newsmen about these little monsters. We'll get the country all up tight."

"Senator," said Congressman Nelson Able, "I think you may have gotten your protocol somewhat twisted. We were not invited here to decide whether the troops were to be brought back home, but rather to learn that they were being brought back and to be told the reason for it."

"I still believe," said Senator Oakes, "that President Henderson would want to know our thoughts. He might not agree with them, but I think that he should hear them."

"That's right, Andy," said the President. "You know that through the years I have listened to you often and almost as often have been fascinated by what you had to say. Which is not to say I agreed with you. Most commonly I don't."

"I am well aware of that," said Oakes, "but it has not stopped me from saying what I think. And I think it's plain damn foolishness to fly back the troops. It's not going to take the total strength of our military might to run down some little chicken-killing monsters.''

''I think the point has been made,'' said Senator Brian Dixon, ''that the monsters will not stay little monsters. The only sensible way for us to tackle them is to run them down before there get to be any more of them and before they have a chance to grow.''

''But how do we know,'' persisted Oakes, ''that they will really grow or increase in numbers? We're taking the word of people who came scurrying back to us because they couldn't face them. And they couldn't face them because they had let down their guard. They had no military and they had no weapons. . . .''

''Now just a minute, Senator,'' protested Congressman Able. ''It's all right for you to make your military speeches up on the Hill. You get a good press there and can impress the public. But this is just among ourselves. We won't be impressed.''

''Gentlemen,'' said the President, ''as I see it, this is all beside the point. With all due deference to the Senator, the military will be brought back home. It will be brought home because the Secretary of Defense and the Chiefs of Staff have told me the forces are needed here. Among ourselves, we discussed it very thoroughly earlier in the day. The feeling was that we cannot take the chance of anything going wrong. We may be aiming at overkill, but that is better than negligence. It may be true that we have been given poor information by the people from the future, but I am not inclined to think so. They have faced the monsters for twenty years and it seems to me that they would know far more of them than we do. I have talked with members of the Academy of Sciences and they tell me, while the characteristics attributed to the monsters may be unusual, that these characteristics do not go contrary to any established biologic rule. So I don't think that you can say there has been any lack of responsibility in the reaching of our decisions. Because of the press of circumstances, we have moved faster than we ordinarily would, but we simply haven't got the time to go at any of this with due deliberation.''

Oakes did not reply, but settled back in his chair, grunting softly to himself.

"There was a report of a monster loose in the Congo," said Congressman Wayne Smith. "Have you, sir, any further information?"

"None," said the President. "We can't be sure one did get through. The reports are unreliable."

"There has been no request for aid to hunt it down?"

"No request," said the President. "Nothing official at all."

"How about the tunnels, sir? The news reports seem to be in some conflict. Some of them, we know, have closed, but I can't seem to get a clear idea of what is going on."

"You probably know as much as we do here, Wayne. Here at home, the Virginia tunnel is closed, of course. Two more were closed without our intervention, one in Wisconsin, the other down in Texas. I suppose those were shut down by the people up in the future when the monsters were coming in too close. Either that or there were malfunctions. Otherwise than that, all the tunnels in the United States still are operating."

"Would you think that the two you mentioned as closing may have done so because all the people had come through? There has to be an end to all these people sometime?"

"We know the Wisconsin tunnel closed because of an attack at the other end. The last of the people who came through told us that. I don't know about the Texas closing. But as to the implied question of all the people through—yes, I would hope that soon the tunnels would start closing because they've done their job."

"Mr. President," said Senator Dixon, "what do you know about the practical side of tunnel building? Can we build the tunnels so the people can go back into the past?"

"I am told we can," said the President. "Our physicists and engineers are working with refugee scientists and engineers right now. The refugees have picked out the sites where the tunnels should be built. One encouraging feature is that not as many tunnels need be built as they used in getting here. There isn't the immediate time pressure to get back into the Miocene that there was in getting here. They built a lot of tunnels up in the future because they knew they must get out quickly if they were to get any appreciable part of the population out at all. Also, as I understand it, there will be no need to build tunnels in all the smaller countries. Transportation can be used to get the people to tunnels several hundred miles away. The same situation applies here. It will be easier to transport the refugees to the tunnels than to build the tunnels. The one thing that is difficult about it is that we must get some tunnels built and the people moving out before the refugees eat us out of house and home."

"The construction of the tunnels, then, isn't beyond our capability? All we need is time, money and labor."

"That is right, Brian. Labor is no problem. The refugees represent a huge and willing labor force and just an hour or so ago I had word from Terry Roberts that our labor people will raise no objection to our using them on what must be viewed as a federal project. Terry assures me that organized labor will cooperate in every way, even to the extent of waiving union rules, if that should be necessary, in the employment of their own members. Labor is no problem. Money is. Even should industry be as willing to go along with us as labor is, a vast amount of retooling will be necessary before we can start fabricating the components for the tunnels. Ordinarily retooling is a time-consuming process and a costly one. The fact that we must get at it immediately and around the clock, and must get it completed within a fraction of the time it would customarily take, makes it expensive beyond anything that can be imagined. When that is done, the components themselves will be costly items. You must remember this is not a problem that we face alone. It is faced by the entire world. The brunt of the work must be borne by the predominantly industrial nations—we, Germany, Russia, France, Britain, China, Japan, and a few others must build the components, not only for ourselves, but for the rest of the world. While we do not need to match the number of tunnels the future people built to get here, we do need to build enough so that there will be a fairly consistent regional distribution when they go back to the Miocene. While the population of the future is not as great as ours, it still is great enough that it must be scattered. The building of a new civilization in the past would be defeated if we dumped too many people in one area. And the building of the components is only part of the industrial problem that we face, although it is the greatest and the most important part. We must also furnish the refugees with the tools and livestock and seed they will need to make a new beginning. Furnishing the tools is going to call for a significant industrial capacity."

145

"Have you talked with anyone in the industrial community?"

"Not personally. Commerce is making some tentative approaches to see what sort of reaction is forthcoming. I have no word as yet. But it seems to me there should be some positive reaction. I should be disappointed if there weren't. This is their neck as well as the rest of us."

Oakes hunched up out of his chair. "Have you any idea yet, Mr. President, what all of this might cost? Any good round figure?"

"No," said the President, "I haven't."

"But it's going to be costly."

"It is going to be costly."

"Maybe a great deal more than the defense budget, which everyone seems so horrified about."

"You want me to say it, of course," said the President, "so I will. Yes, it is going to be more costly than the defense budget, many times more costly. It will be even more costly than a war. It will maybe break us. It may bankrupt the world, but what would you have us do? Go out and shoot down all the refugees? That would solve the problem. Is that a solution you would like?"

Grumbling, Oakes let himself sink back into the chair.

"One thing has occurred to me," said Able. "There is just the possibility that no matter what it costs us, we may get value received. The refugees come from a time period where many technological problems have been worked out, new approaches have been developed. One thing that has been mentioned is fusion power. We are nowhere near that yet; it may take us years to get there. If we had fusion power that would be a great leap forward. Undoubtedly there are many others. I would assume that, in return for what we propose to do for them, they'd be willing to acquaint us with the basics of these technological advances. . . ."

"It would ruin us," Oakes said wrathfully. "It would finish up the job they've started. Take fusion power, for instance. There, gentlemen, in the twinkling of an eye, the gas and oil and coal industries would go down the drain."

"And," said Able, "I suppose the medical profession as well if up in the future they had found the cause and cure of cancer."

146

Dixon said, "What the Congressman says is true. If we had the advantages of all their scientific and technological advances, perhaps their social and political advances, that have been made, or will be made, in the next five hundred years, we would be much better off than we are today. To whom, I wonder, would the new knowledge and principles belong? To the man who was able to acquire the information, by whatever means? Or to the governments? Or to the world at large? And if to the governments and the world, how would it be handled or implemented? It seems to me that, at best, we would have many thorny problems to work out."

"This is all in the future," said Congressman Smith. "It is speculative at the moment. Right now, it seems to me, we have two immediate problems. We have to somehow dispose of the monsters and we must do whatever is possible to send the future people back to the Miocene. Is this the way you read it, Mr. President?"

"Exactly," said the President, "as I read it."

"I understand," Oakes rumbled, "that the Russian ambassador is coming over to have a powwow with you."

"You were not supposed to know that, Andy."

"Well, you know how it is, Mr. President. You stay up on the Hill long enough and you get a lot of pipelines. You get told a lot of things. Even things you were not supposed to know."

"It's no secret," said the President. "I have no idea why he's coming. We are trying to work closely with all the governments in this matter. I have had phone conversations with a number of heads of state, including the Russian head of state. I take it that the ambassador's visit is no more than an extension of these talks."

"Perhaps," said Oakes. "Perhaps. I just tend to get a mite nervous when the Russians become too interested in anything at all."

37

THERE was something in the hazel thicket at the edge of the tiny cornfield—a vague sense of a presence, a tantalizing outline that never quite revealed itself. Something lurked there, waiting. Sergeant Gordy Clark was quite sure of that. Just how he knew he could not be sure. But he was sure—or almost sure. Some instinct born out of hundreds of patrols into enemy country, something gained by the sharp, hard objectivity that was necessary for an old soldier to keep himself alive while others died—something that he nor no one else could quite define told him there was a lurker in the thicket.

He lay silent, almost unbreathing in his effort to be quiet and still, stretched out on the little ridge that rose above the cornfield, with his rocket launcher steadied on an ancient, rotted log and the cross-hairs centered on the thicket. It could be a dog, he told himself, or a child, perhaps even nothing, but he could not bring himself to think that it was nothing.

The drooping sumac bush bent close above him, shielding him from the view of whatever might be in the thicket. He could hear the faint mutter of the mountain brook that ran just beyond the cornfield, and from up the hollow hugged between the hills, where the farm buildings were located, came the senseless cackling of a hen.

There was no sign of any other member of the patrol. He knew several of them must be close, but they were being careful not to betray their presence. They were regulars, every one of them, and they knew their business. They could move through these woods like shadows. They would make no noise, disturb no brush or branch to give away their presence.

The sergeant smiled grimly to himself. They were good men. He had trained them all. The captain thought that he had been the one who had trained them, but it had not been the captain. It had been Sergeant Gordon Fairfield Clark who had beaten their business into them. They all hated him, of course, and he'd have it no other way. For out of hatred could sometimes come respect. Fear or respect, he thought—either one would serve. There were some of them, perhaps not now, but sometime in the past—had cherished the fantasy of putting a bullet through his skull. There must have been opportunities, but they had never done it. For they needed him, the sergeant told himself—although not really him, of course, but the hatred that they had for him. There was nothing like a good strong hatred for a man to cling to.

The farmer at the buildings up the hollow thought he had seen something. He couldn't tell what it was, but it had been awful, the glimpse he had gotten of it. A sort of thing that he had never seen before. Something that no man could imagine. The farmer had shivered as he talked.

The thing that had been in the thicket came out. It came out with a rush so fast that it seemed to blur. Then, as quickly as it had moved, it stopped. It stood in the little open space of ground between the thicket and the corn.

The sergeant caught his breath and his guts turned over, but even so he swiveled the launcher barrel around so that the cross hairs centered on the great paunch of the monster and his finger began the steady squeeze.

Then it was gone. The cross hairs centered on nothing except the ragged clump of brush beyond the cornfield's edge. The sergeant didn't stir. He lay looking through the sight, but his finger slacked off from the trigger.

The monster had not moved. He was sure of that. It had simply disappeared. One microsecond there, the next microsecond gone. It could not move that fast. When it had come out of the thicket there had been a blur of rapid movement. This time there had been no blur.

Sergeant Clark raised his head, levered himself to his knees. He put up a hand and wiped his face and was astonished to find that his hand came away greasy wet. He'd not been aware that he had been sweating.

38

FYODOR MOROZOV was a good diplomat and decent man, the two not being incompatible, and he hated what he had to do. Besides, he told himself, he knew Americans and it simply would not work. It would, of course, embarrass them and point out their sins for all the world to see and, under ordinary circumstances, he would not have been averse to this. But under present conditions, he knew, the Americans (or anyone else, for that matter) were in no position to observe the niceties of diplomatic games, and because of this, there was no way one could gauge reaction.

The President was waiting for him when he was ushered in and beside the President, as was to be expected, stood the Secretary of State. The President was all open blandness, but Thornton Williams, Fyodor could see, was a somewhat puzzled man, although he was doing an excellent job of hiding it.

When they had shaken hands and sat down, the President opened the conversation. "It's always good to see you, Mr. Ambassador," he said, "for any reason, or even for no reason. But tell me, is there something we can do for you?"

"My government," said Fyodor, "has asked me to confer with your government, as unofficially as our official positions can make possible, concerning a matter of security which I would assume is of some concern to both of us, in fact, to everyone."

He paused and they waited for him to go on. They did not

respond; they asked no question; they were no help at all.

"It is the matter," he said, "of the alien monster that escaped from the Congo tunnel. There is no question, knowing what we do, that the monsters must be hunted down. Since the Congo does not have sufficient military or police forces to accomplish this, my government is offering to supply an expeditionary force and we are about to sound out both Britain and France and perhaps other nations as well to determine if they might want to contribute to a joint expeditionary force against the monster."

"Certainly, Ambassador," said Williams, "your government does not feel compelled to seek our permission to embark upon so neighborly an undertaking. I would imagine that you are prepared to make guarantees that you'll withdraw all forces immediately the monster has been taken."

"Of course we are."

"Then I fail to grasp your point."

"There is also," said Fyodor, "the matter of the monster, or the monsters—I understood that now there are a number of them—on your own territory. We are prepared to make the same offer to you as we will make the Congo."

"You mean," said the President, amused, "that you would be willing to lend us some of your forces to hunt down the monsters."

"We would go, I think," said the ambassador, "somewhat beyond the word you use—willing. I would think that unless you can guarantee absolute effectiveness in containing and disposing of the monsters, we might possibly insist. This is not a national matter; the international community is concerned. The creatures must be obliterated. If you can't accomplish this, then you must accept any help that's offered."

"You know, of course," said Williams, "that we are bringing home our troops."

"I know that, Mr. Secretary, but the question is how quickly can you bring them home. Our military people estimate it will take you thirty days at least and that may not be fast enough. There also is the question of whether you have personnel enough to cover the required territory."

The President said, "I can assure you that we appreciate your concern."

"It is the position of my government," said Fyodor, "that

while naturally you wish to use your own troops, many more men would be placed upon the ground and more quickly if you would accept the aid that we offer and which I am sure other nations as well would offer if you made known your willingness. . . ."

"Mr. Ambassador," said the President, interrupting, "I am certain you know better than to come to us with such an impudent suggestion. If there had been genuine good will on the part of your government, surely you are aware that a different approach would have been employed. There is no question in my mind that the sole purpose of this call is to embarrass us. In that, of course, you've failed. We are not in the least embarrassed."

"I am delighted that you're not," said Fyodor, unruffled. "We thought that it was only the decent thing to approach you first, in private."

"I assume," said Williams, "you mean you now will bring the matter up before the UN, where you'll seek to embarrass us in public."

"You gentlemen," said the ambassador, "persist in placing a wrong interpretation upon the matter. It is true, of course, that our countries have had their differences in the past. We have not always seen exactly eye to eye. Under present circumstances, however, the entire world need stand together. It is only with this thought that we bring the matter forward. It is quite clear to us, if it is not to you, that solving the monster problem quickly is in the international interest and that it is your duty to accept such aid as may be needed. We should be reluctant to report to the United Nations that you neglect your duty."

"We would not attempt," said Williams stiffly, "to suggest what you might tell the UN."

"If you should decide to accept our offer," said the ambassador, "it would be agreeable to us to leave the initiative with you. If you should ask other nations—perhaps Canada, Britain, France and us—to supply the additional forces that you need, there need be nothing said concerning this particular conversation. The newsmen, of course, will know that I am here and will ask me about it, but I shall tell them it was only a part of the continuing discussion which is going on between our two countries concerning the refugee situation. That sort of answer, it seems to me, would be a logical one and probably acceptable.''

"I suppose," said the President, "that you will want an answer to relay to your government."

"Not necessarily now," said Fyodor. "We would imagine you might want to deliberate upon it. The UN does not meet until tomorrow noon."

"I imagine that if we asked some of our friends among the community of nations to supply us forces and did not include your government among them, you would feel slighted and be indignantly offended.''

"I cannot speak to that with any surety, but I would presume we might be."

"It seems to me," said the Secretary of State, "that all of this is no more than official mischief-making. I have known you for some years and have held a high regard for you. You have been here among us for three years, or is it four—more than three years, anyhow—and surely you have grown to know us in that length of time. I think that your heart may not be entirely in these proceedings."

Fyodor Morozov rose slowly to his feet. "I have delivered the message from my government," he said. "Thank you both for seeing me."

39

IN New York, in Chicago, in Atlanta mobs hurled themselves against police lines. The signs read: WE DIDN'T ASK THEM TO COME. They read: WE HAVE LITTLE ENOUGH AS IT IS. They read: WE REFUSE TO STARVE. The crowds threw objects, stones, bricks, tin cans battered into tin-shinny pucks so they had cutting edges, plastic bags filled with human excrement. The ghetto areas were filled with shouting and with violence. Some died; many were injured. Bonfires were kindled. Houses burned and when fire rigs tried to reach the blazes, they were stopped by barricades. Great areas were given over to looting.

In little towns throughout the country grim-faced men talked—sitting on benches in front of general stores, filling stations, feed stores, stopping at street corners, gathering for coffee in the corner drugstore, waiting their turns in barbershops. They said to one another, among themselves, bewildered: It don't seem right, somehow. It don't seem possible. It ain't like the old days, when one knew what was going on. There ain't no telling, these days, what is about to happen, what will happen next. There is too much new-fangled now. The old days are going fast. There is nothing left for a man to hang to. . . . They said judiciously: Of course, if it is the way they say, we got to do our best for them. You heard the President say it last night. Children of our children. That is what he said. Although I don't know how we are going to do it. Not with taxes what they are. We can't pay no more taxes than we are and them tunnels are about to cost a mint. Taxes on everything you buy. On everything you do. On everything you own. Seems no matter how hard a man may scratch he can't keep ahead of taxes. . . . They said sanctimoniously: That preacher down in Nashville hit it on the head. If a man loses his religion he has lost everything worthwhile. He has nothing left to live for. You lose the Good Book and you have lost it all. It don't seem possible that even in five hundred years men would have given up their God. It's the evil in the world today, right now, that made it possible. It's big-city living. The meanness of big-city living. Out here you could never lose your God. No, sir. He's with you all the time. You feel Him in the wind. You see Him in the color of the eastern sky just before the break of dawn. You sense Him in the hush of evening. I feel sorry for these people from the future. I do feel purely sorry for them. They don't know what they lost. . . . They said angrily of the riots: They ought to shoot them down. I wouldn't fool around with stuff like that. Not for a minute would I. Those people, some of them ain't never done a lick of work in all their entire lives. They just stand there with their hands out. You can't tell me, if a man really wants to work, or a woman either, they can't find a job. Out here we scratch and dig and sweat and we get next to nothing, but we don't riot, we don't burn, we don't stand with hands out. . . . They said of the young people with the signs in Lafayette Park: If they want to go to the Miocene or whatever this place is, why don't we let them go? We won't never miss them. We would be better off without them. . . . The village banker said, with ponderous judiciousness: Mark my word, we'll be lucky if these future folks don't ruin the entire country. Yes, sir, the entire country; maybe the entire world. The dollar will be worth nothing and prices will go up. . . . And inevitably they got around to it, whispering the blackest of their thoughts: You just wait and see. It's a Commie plot, I tell you. A dirty Commie plot. I don't know how they worked it, but when the wash comes out, we'll find these Russians at the bottom of it. . . .

There was marching in the land, a surge toward Washington—by hitchhiking, by bus, by old beat-up clunkers of cars. An inward streaming of the countercultural young. Some of them reached the city before the fall of night and marched with banners saying: Back To The Miocene; Bring On

The Sabretooths! Others continued through the night or rested in the night to continue with first light, sleeping in haystacks or on park benches, wolfing hamburgers, seeking out alliances, talking in hushed tones around campfires.

Other bands marched as well in the streets of Washington, bands in the center of which were young men staggering under the weight of heavy crosses, stumbling and falling, then staggering up again to continue on their way. Some wore crowns of thorns, with blood trickling down their foreheads. Late in the afternoon a furious fight broke out in Lafayette Park when an indignant crowd, among them many of the hopefully Miocene-bound youngsters, moved to stop a crucifixion, with the victim already lashed to the cross and the hole half dug for its planting. Police charged in and after a bloody fifteen minutes cleared the park. When all were gone, four crudely fashioned crosses were gathered up and carted off. "These kids are crazy," said one panting officer. "I wouldn't give you a dime for the entire lot of them."

Senator Andrew Oakes phoned Grant Wellington. "Now is the time," he said in a conspiratorial voice, "to lie extremely low. Don't say a word. Don't even look as if you were interested. The situation, you might say, is fluid. There is nothing set. No one knows which way the cat will jump. There is something going on. The Russian was at the White House this morning and that bodes no good for anyone. Something we don't understand is very much afoot."

Clinton Chapman phoned Reilly Douglas. "You know anything, Reilly?"

"Nothing except that there really is time travel and we have the blueprints for it."

"You have seen the blueprints?"

"No, I haven't. It all is under wraps. No one is saying anything. The scientists who talked with the future people aren't talking."

"But you. . . ."

"I know, Clint. I'm the Attorney General, but, hell, in a thing like this that doesn't count for anything. This is top secret. A few of the Academy crowd and that is all. Not even the military, and even if the military wanted it, I have my doubts . . ."

"But they have to let someone know. You can't build a thing until you know."

"Sure, how to build it, but that is all. Not how it works. Not why it works. Not the principle."

"What the hell difference does that make?"

"I should think it would," said Douglas. "I, personally, would be distrustful of building something I didn't understand."

"You say it is time travel. No doubt of that, it is really time travel."

"No doubt at all," said Douglas.

"Then there's a mint in it," said Chapman, "and I mean to. . . ."

"But if it only works one way—"

"It has to work both ways," said Chapman. "That's what my people tell me."

"It will take a lot of financing," said Douglas.

"I've talked to a lot of people," said Chapman. "People I can trust. Some of them are interested. Enough of them. Definitely interested. They see the possibilities. There'll be no lack of funds if we can put it through."

Judy Gray got on the plane and found her seat. She looked out the window, saw the scurrying trucks—saw them mistily and quickly put up a hand to wipe her eyes. She said to herself, almost lovingly, through clenched teeth: "The son of a bitch. The dirty son of a bitch!"

40

TOM MANNING spoke guardedly into the phone. "Steve," he said, "I have been hearing things."

"Put them on the wire, Tom," said Wilson. "That is why you are there. Put them on the wire for the glory of dear old Global News."

"Now," said Manning, "that you've had occasion to show off your shallow sense of humor, shall we get down to business?"

"If this is a ploy," said Wilson, "to trick me into seeming confirmation of some rumor you have heard, you know that it won't work."

"You know me better than that, Steve."

"That's the trouble, I do know you."

"All right, then," said Manning, "if that's the way of it, let's start at the beginning. The President had the Russian ambassador in this morning. . . ."

"The President didn't have him him. He came in on his own. The ambassador made a statement to the press. You know about that."

"Sure, we know what the ambassador said and what you said in this afternoon's briefing, which, I might say, added very little light to the situation. But no one in town, no one in his right mind, that is, buys what either of you said."

"I'm sorry about that, Tom. I told all I knew."

"OK," said Manning. "I'll take your word for that. It's just possible that you weren't told. But there's a very nasty story being whispered up at the UN in New York. At least, it was whispered to our man up there. I don't know how much farther it has gone. Our man didn't put it on the wire. He phoned me and I told him to hold it until I talked with you.''

''I don't have the least idea, Tom, of what you're talking about. I had honestly assumed the ambassador told all that could be told. There have been some conversations with Moscow and it sounded reasonable. The President didn't tell me differently. We mentioned it, I guess, but we didn't talk about it. There were so many other things.''

''All right, then,'' said Manning, ''here's the story as I heard it. Morozov talked to Williams and the President and offered troops to help hunt down the monster and the offer was rejected. . . .''

''Tom, how good is your source? How sure are you of this?''

''Not sure at all. It's what our man at the UN was told this afternoon.''

''You're talking about Max Hale. He's your man up there.''

''One of the best,'' said Manning. ''He's fairly good at sorting out the truth.''

''Yes, he is. I remember him from Chicago days.''

''Hale's informant told him that tomorrow the UN will be told of our refusal and a demand made that we be forced to accept troops from other nations. It'll be said that we are negligent in not accepting them.''

''The old squeeze play,'' said Wilson.

''And that's not all of it. If other troops are not accepted and the monsters can't be controlled, then, the UN will be told, the entire area must be nuclearly destroyed. The world can't take a chance. . . .''

''Wait a minute,'' said Wilson quickly. ''You're not putting this on the wires, you say?''

''Not yet. Probably never. I hope that it is never. That's the reason I phoned. If Hale heard it, there's a likelihood someone else will hear it and, sure as God, it will get on a wire or be published somewhere.''

''There's no truth in it,'' said Wilson. ''I am sure of it. Christ, we're all in this together. For the moment, political power plays should be set aside. Or it seems to me they should. Tom, I simply can't believe it."

"You know nothing of this? Of any of it? There hasn't been a breath?"

"Not a breath," said Wilson.

"You know," said Manning, "I wouldn't have your job, Steve. Not for a million dollars."

"You'll hold off, Tom. You'll give us a little time to check."

"Of course. Only if the pressure gets too great. Only if someone else—I'll let you know."

"Thanks, Tom. Someday. . . ."

"Someday, when this is all over," said Manning, "we'll go off in some dark corner in an obscure bar, where no one possibly can find us, and we'll hang one on."

"I'll stand the drinks," said Wilson. "All the drinks."

After hanging up, he sat slumped. Just when another day was about to end, he thought. But hell, some days never ended. They just kept on and on. Yesterday and today had not been two days, but a nightmare-haunted eternity that seemed, when one thought of it, to have no reality at all. Judy gone, kids marching in the street, the business community bitching loudly because it was prevented from using the economic disruption to go out and make a killing, pulpit-thumping preachers hellbent to make another kind of killing, monsters running in the hills and the future still emptying its humanity upon this moment in the time track.

His eyelids slid down and stuck and he forced himself erect. He had to get some sleep tonight—he had to find the time to get some sleep.

Maybe Judy had the right idea. Just up and walk away from it. Although, he told himself, quite honestly, there still remained the question of what she'd walked away from. He missed her—gone no more than an hour or two and he was missing her. Quite suddenly, he realized he'd been missing her all day. Even while she still had been here, he had been missing her. Knowing she would be leaving, he had started missing her. Maybe, he thought, he should have asked her once again to stay, but there hadn't been the time and he'd not known how to do it—at least he had not know how to do it gracefully and you did things gracefully or you did them not at all. More than likely, had he known, she'd not have listened to him.

He picked up the phone. "Kim, you still there? I'll need to see the President. It is rather urgent. The first chance you have to squeeze me in."

"It may be some time, Steve," she said. "There is a cabinet meeting."

41

SERGEANT GORDON FAIRFIELD CLARK said to Colonel Eugene Dawson, "I had it in my sights and then it wasn't there. It disappeared. It went away. I'm sure it didn't move. I saw it move before it stopped. It blurred when it moved. Like a cartoonist drawing something moving fast, lettering in a SWISH, but this was without a swish. When it disappeared there wasn't any swish. The first time I could see that it was moving. But not when I had it in my sights. It didn't move then. It didn't blur. It didn't swish."

"It saw you, Sergeant," said the colonel.

"I would think not, sir. I was well hidden. I didn't move. I moved the launcher barrel a couple of inches. That was all."

"One of your men, then."

"Sir, all those men I trained myself. No one sees them, no one hears them."

"It saw something. Or heard something. It sensed some danger and then it disappeared. You're sure about this disappearance, Sergeant?"

"Colonel, I am sure."

Dawson was sitting on a fallen log. He reached down and picked up a small twig from the duff of the forest floor, began breaking it and rebreaking it, reducing the twig to bits of wood. Clark stayed squatting to one side, using the launcher, its butt resting on the ground, as a partial support to his squatting pose.

"Sergeant," Dawson said, "I don't know what the hell we're

going to do about all this. I don't know what the army's going to do. You find one of these things and before you can whap it, it is gone. We can handle them. I am sure of that. Even when they get big and rough and mean, like the people from the future say they will, we still can handle them. We've got the firepower. We have the sophistication. If they'd line up and we'd line up and they came at us, we could clobber them. We have more and better armaments than the people of future had and we can do the job. But not when they're trying to keep clear of us, not in this kind of terrain. We could bomb ten thousand acres flat and get, maybe, one of them. God knows how much else we'd kill, including people. We haven't the time or manpower to evacuate the people so that we can bomb. We got to hunt these monsters down, one by one. . . ."

"But even when we hunt them down, sir. . . ."

"Yes, I know. But say that you are lucky. Say you bag one now and then. There still will be hundreds of them hatching and in a week or so, a month or so, thousands of them hatching. And the first ones growing bigger and meaner all the time. And while we hunt for them, they wipe out a town or two, an army camp or two. . . ."

"Sir," said Sergeant Clark, "it is worse than Vietnam ever was. And Vietnam was hairy."

The colonel got up from the log. "There hasn't nothing beat us yet," he said. "Nothing has ever beat us all the way. It won't this time. But we have to find out how to do it. All the firepower in the world, all the sophistication in the world is of no use to you until you can find something to aim the firepower and the sophistication at and it stays put until you pull the trigger."

The sergeant got to his feet, tucked the launcher underneath his arm. "Well, back to work," he said.

"Have you seen a photographer around here?"

"A photographer?" said the sergeant. "What photographer? I ain't seen no photographer."

"He said his name was Price. With some press association. He was messing around. I put the run on him."

"If I happen onto him," said the sergeant, "I'll tie a knot into his tail."

42

THE Reverend Jake Billings was in conference with Ray MacDonald, formerly his assistant public relations manager, who had been appointed, within the last twelve hours, to the post of crusade operations chief.

"I really do not think, Ray," said the Reverend Billings, "that this business of crucifixion will advance our cause. It strikes me as being rather crude and it could backlash against us. As witness what one paper had to say of the attempt at Washington. . . ."

"You mean someone has already gotten around to editorializing on it? I had not expected such prompt reaction."

"The reaction is not good," said the Reverend Billings, with some unaccustomed heat. "The editorial called it a cheap trick and a pantywaisted effort. The young man's arms, it turns out, were fastened to the crossbar with thongs—not nails, but thongs. The entire editorial, of course, is in a somewhat facetious vein, but nevertheless. . . ."

"But they are wrong," MacDonald said.

"You mean that you used nails!"

"No, that's not what I mean. I mean that thongs were the way that it was done. The Romans ordinarily did not use nails. . . ."

"You are trying to tell me that the Gospels erred?"

"No, I'm not trying to tell you that. What I am saying is that ordinarily—ordinarily, mind you, perhaps not always—the arms were tied, not nailed. We did some research on it and. . . ."

"Your research is no concern of mine," said Billings icily. "What I do care about is that you gave some smart-assed editorial writer the chance to poke fun at us. And even if that had not happened, I think the whole idea stinks. You didn't check with me. How come you didn't check with me?"

"You were busy, Jake. You told me to do my best. You told me I was the man who could come up with ideas and I did come up with ideas."

"I had this call from Steve Wilson," Billings said. "He chewed me out. There is no doubt that official Washington—the White House, at least—is solidly against us. When he gets around to it, Wilson will brand us as sensationalists. He brushed us off contemputuously in his press briefing this afternoon. That was before this silly crucifixion business. Next time around, he'll blast us out of the water."

"But we have a lot of people with us. You go out to the countryside, to the little towns. . . ."

"Yes, I know. The rednecks. They'll be for us, sure, but how long do you think it is before redneck opinion can have any significant impact? What about the influential pastors in the big city churches? Can you imagine what the Reverend Dr. Angus Windsor will tell his congregation and the newspapers and the world? He's the one who started all of this, but he'll not go along with solemn young men packing crosses through the street and getting crucified on a public square. For years I have tried to conduct my ministry with dignity and now it's been pulled down to the level of street brawling. I have you to thank for this and. . . ."

"It's not too different," protested MacDonald, "from the stunts we've used before. Good old circus stuff. Good old show biz. It's what you built the business on."

"But with restraint."

"Not too much restraint. Skywriting and parades and miles of billboards. . . ."

"Legitimate advertising," said Billings. "Honest advertising. A great American tradition. The mistake you made was to go out in the streets. You don't know about the streets. You ran up against the experts there. These Miocene kids know about the streets. They have been there. they have lived there. You had

166

two strikes on you before you started out. What made you think you could compete with them?"

"All right, then, what shall we do? The streets are out, you say. So we pull off the streets. Then what do we do? How do we get attention?"

The Reverend Jake Billings stared at the wall with glassy eyes. "I don't know," he said. "I purely do not know. I don't think it makes much difference what we do. I think that gurgling noise you hear is our crusade going down the drain."

43

IT was the dog that did it. Bentley Price hadn't had a drink all day. The road was a narrow, winding mountain road, and Bentley, exasperated beyond endurance at what had happened to him, was driving faster than he should. After hours of hunting for it, he had finally found the camp—a very temporary camp by the looks of it, with none of the meticulous neatness of the usual army camp, simply a stopping place in a dense patch of woods beside a stream that came brawling down the valley. Filled with a deep sense of duty done and perseverance paying off, he had slung cameras around his neck and gone plodding toward the largest of the tents and had almost reached it when the colonel had come out to stop his further progress. Who the hell are you, the colonel had asked and where do you think you're going? I am the Global News, Bentley had told him, and I am out here to take some pictures of this monster hunt. I tell the city editor it isn't worth the time, but he disagrees with me and it's no skin off my nose no matter where I'm sent, so leave us get the lead out and do some monster hunting so I can get some pictures.

You're off limits, mister, the colonel had told him. You are way off limits, in more ways than one. I don't know how you got this far. Didn't someone try to stop you? Sure, said Bentley, up the road a ways. A couple of soldier boys. But I pay no attention to them. I never pay attention to someone who tries to stop me. I got work to do and I can't fool around.

And then the colonel had thrown him out of there. He had

spoken in a clipped, military voice and had been very icy-eyed. We've got trouble enough, he said, without some damn fool photographer mucking around and screwing up the detail. If you don't leave under your own power, I'll have you escorted out. While he was saying this, Bentley snapped a camera up and took a picture of him. That made the situation even worse, and Bentley, with his usual quick perception, could see his cause had worsened, so had beat a dignified retreat to avoid escort. When he had passed the soldier boys who had tried to stop him they had yelled at him and thumbed their noses. Bentley had slowed down momentarily, debating whether to go back and reason with them, then had thought better of it. They ain't worth the time, he told himself.

Now the dog.

The dog came bursting out of high weeds and brush that grew along the road. His ears were laid back, his tail tucked in and he was kiyodeling in pure, blind panic. The dog was close and the car traveling much too fast. Bentley jerked the wheel. The car veered off the road, smashed through a clump of brush. The tires screamed as Bentley hit the brakes. The nose of the car slammed hard into a huge walnut tree and stopped with a shuddering impact. The left-hand door flew open and Bentley, who held a lofty disdain for such copouts as seat belts, was thrown free. The camera which he wore on a strap around his neck, described a short arc and brought up against his ear, dealing him a blow that made his head ring as if there were a bell inside it. He landed on his back and rolled, wound up on hands and knees. He surged erect and found that he had ended up on the edge of the road.

Standing in the middle of the road was a monster. Bentley knew it was a monster, he had seen two of them only yesterday. But this one was small, no bigger than a Shetland pony. Which did not mean the horror of it was any less.

But Bentley was of different fiber from other men. He did not gulp; his gut did not turn over. His hands came up with swift precision, grabbed the camera firmly, brought it to his eye. The monster was framed in the finder and his finger pressed the button. The camera clicked and as it clicked the monster disappeared.

Bentley lowered the camera and let loose of it. His head still rang from the blow upon the ear. His clothes were torn; a gaping

169

rent in a trouser leg revealed one knobby knee. His right hand was bloody from where his palm had scraped across some gravel. Behind him the car creaked slightly as twisted metal settled slowly into place. The motor pinged and sizzled as water from the broken radiator ran across hot metal.

Off in the distance the still-running dog was yipping frantically. In a tree up the hillside an excited squirrel chattered with machine-gun intensity. The road was empty. A monster had been there. From where he stood, Bentley could see its tracks printed in the dust. But it was no longer there.

Bentley limped out into the road, stared both up and down it. There was nothing on the road.

It was there, said Bentley stubbornly to himself. I had it in the finder. It was there when I shot the picture. It wasn't until the shutter clicked that it disappeared. Doubt assailed him. Had it been there or not when he'd shot the picture? Was it on the film? Had he been robbed of a photo by its disappearance?

Thinking about it, it seemed that it had been there, but he could not be sure.

He turned about and started limping down the road as rapidly as he could. There was one way to find out. He had to get to a phone, he had to somehow get a car. He must get back to Washington.

44

"WE have made three contacts with the monsters," Sandburg said. "There are yet to be results. No one has had a chance to fire at them. They disappear and that's the end of it."

"You mean," said Thorton Williams, "that they duck away. . . ."

"No, I don't mean that," said the Secretary of Defense. "They just aren't there, is all. The men who saw them swore they didn't move at all. They were there and then they weren't. The observers, all reporting independently, not knowing of the other reports, have been very sure of that. One man could be wrong in his observation; it's possible that two could be. It seems impossible that three observers could err on exactly the same point."

"Have you, has the military, any theory, any idea of what is going on?"

"None," said Sandburg. "It must be a new defensive adaptation that they have developed. These creatures, as you all by now must understand, are very much on the defensive. They know they have to survive. For the good of the species, they can't take any chances. Cornered, I suppose that they would fight, but only if they were cornered and there was no way out. Apparently they have come up with something new under this sort of situation. We have talked with Dr. Isaac Wolfe, the refugee biologist who probably knows more about the monsters than any other man, and this business of disappearing is something he has never heard of. He suggests, simply as a guess, that it may be an ability that only the juvenile monsters have. A sort of juvenile defense mechanism. It may have gone on unobserved up in the future because the people up there had little opportunity to observe the juveniles; they had their hands full fighting off the adult monsters.''

''How are you doing with getting men into the area?'' asked the President.

''I haven't any figures,'' said Sandburg, ''but we're piling them in as fast as we can get them there. The refugee camps have formed their own caretaking committees and that takes off some of the pressure, frees some troops. Agriculture and Welfare are taking over a lot of the transport that is needed to get food and other necessities into the camps and that, as well, has freed military personnel. We expect the first overseas transport planes to begin landing sometime tonight and that will give us more men.''

'':Morozov was in this morning,'' said Williams, ''with an offer to supply us men. In fact, he rather insisted upon it. We, of course, rejected the offer. But it does raise a point. Should we, perhaps, ask for some assistance from Canada, perhaps Mexico, maybe Britain, France, Germany—others of our friends?''

''Possibly we could use some of their forces,'' said Sandburg. ''I'd like to talk with the Chiefs of Staff and get their reactions. What we need, and haven't been able to manage, are some rather substantial forces, both north and south—down in Georgia, say, and in upstate New York. We should try to seal off the monsters' spread, if they are spreading, and I suppose that is their intention. If we can contain them, we can handle them.''

''If they stand still,'' said the President.

''That is right,'' said Sandburg. ''If they stand still.''

''Maybe we should move on to something else,'' suggested the President. ''Reilly, I think you have something to report.''

''I'm still not too solid on it yet,'' said Reilly Douglas, ''but it is a matter that should be discussed. Frankly, I am inclined to think there may be a rather tricky legal question involved and I've had no chance to go into that aspect of it. Clinton Chapman came to see me last night. I think most of you know Clint.''

He looked around the table. Many of the men nodded their heads.

"He came to me," said Douglas, "and since then has phoned three or four times and we had lunch today. I suppose some of you know that we were roommates at Harvard and have been friends ever since. I suppose that's why he contacted me. On his first approach he proposed that he, himself, would take over the building of the tunnels, financing the cost with no federal funds involved. In return he would continue in ownership of them once the future people had been transported back to the Miocene and would be licensed to operate them. Since then. . . ."

"Reilly," Williams interrupted, "I can't quite understand why anyone would want to own them. What in the world could be done with them? The time force, or whatever it is, as I understand it, operates in only one direction—into the past."

Douglas shook his head. "Clint won't buy that. He has talked with his research men—and the research staff he has is probably one of the best in the world—and they have assured him that if there is such a thing as time travel, it can be made to operate in two directions—both into the past and futureward. As a matter of fact, they told him it would seem easier to operate it futureward than into the past because time's natural flow is futureward."

Williams blew out a gusty breath. "I don't know," he said. "It has a dirty sound to it. Could we conscientiously turn over two-way time travel, if two-way time travel is possible, to any one man or any group of men? Think of the ways it could be used. . . ."

"I talked to Clint about this at lunch," said Douglas. "I explained to him that any such operation, if it were possible, would have to be very strictly controlled. Commissions would have to be set up to formulate a time travel code, Congress would have to legislate. Not only that, but the code and the legislation would have to be worldwide; there would have to be some international agreement, and you can imagine how long that might take. Clint agreed to all of this, said he realized it would be necessary. The man is quite obsessed with the idea. As an old friend, I tried to talk him out of it, but he still insists he wants to go ahead. If he is allowed to do it, that is. At first he planned to finance it on his own, but apparently is beginning to realize the kind of money that would be involved. As I understand it, he is now very quietly trying to put togethei a consortium to take over the project.''

Sandburg frowned. ''I would say no on impulse. Time travel would have to be studied closely. It's something we've never thought seriously of before. We'd have to think it through.''

''It could have military applications,'' said Williams. ''I'm not just sure what they would be.''

''International agreements, with appropriate safeguards, would have to be set up to keep it from being used militarily,'' said the President. ''And if these agreements should fail at some time in the future, I can't see that it would make much difference who held the license for time travel. National needs would always take precedence. No matter how it goes, time travel is something that we're stuck with. It's something we have to face. We have to make the best of it.''

''You favor Clint's proposal, Mr. President?'' Douglas asked in some surprise. ''When I talked with you. . . .''

''I wouldn't go so far as to say I favored it,'' said the President. ''But under the situation we face, it seems to me we should consider all possibilities or proposals. We are going to be hard pressed to find the kind of money or credit that is needed to build the tunnels. Not only us, but the world. Perhaps the rest of the world even more than us.''

''That brings us to another point,'' said Williams, ''I would suppose Chapman and his consortium are proposing only the tunnels in the United States.''

''I can't say as to that,'' said Douglas. ''I would imagine that if Chapman could put his consortium together it might include some foreign money, and agreements could be made with other nations. I can't see a country like the Congo or Portugal or Indonesia turning its back on someone who wants to build its tunnels. Other nations might be hesitant, but if we went along with the plan and a couple of the other major nations joined us, say Germany or France, then most of the others, I would think, would follow. After all, if everyone else were going ahead with the plan, no nation would want to be left out in the cold without a tunnel.''

''This is going to cost a lot of money,'' said Manfred

Franklin, Secretary of the Treasury. "Tunnels for the entire world would run into billions."

"There are a lot of gamblers in the financial world," observed Ben Cunningham, of Agriculture. "But mostly it is smart gambling, smart money. Chapman must be fairly certain of himself. Do you imagine he may know something that we don't know?"

Douglas shook his head. "I am inclined to think not. He has this assurance, you see, from his research people, principally the physicists, I understand, that if time travel is possible it has to be a two-way street. By now it is apparent that it is possible. You see, this is the first new idea, the first really new idea that has real technological and engineering potential, that has come along in fifty years or more. Clint and his gang want to get in on the ground floor."

"The question," said Williams, "is should we let them."

"Much as we may regret to do so," said the President, "we may have to. If we refused, word would be leaked to the public and you can imagine what the public reaction would be. Oh, a few would oppose it, but they would be drowned out by those who would see it as allowing someone to pay a huge expenditure that otherwise would come out of the treasury and be paid by taxes. Frankly, gentlemen, we may find ourselves in a position where opposing the consortium would be political suicide."

"You don't seem to be too upset about it," said Williams somewhat acidly.

"When you have been in politics as long as I have been, Thornton, you don't gag too easily at anything that comes up. You learn to be practical. You weigh things in balance. I admit privately that I gag considerably at this, but I am politically practical to the point where I can recognize it may not be possible to fight it. There are times when you simply cannot take pot shots at Santa Claus."

"I still don't like it," said Williams.

"Nor do I," said Sandburg.

"It would be a solution," said Franklin. "Labor is ready to go along with us in the emergency. If the financial interests of the world would go along with us, which is actually what would happen under this consortium setup, our basic problem would be solved. We still have to feed the people from the future, but I understand we can do that longer than we had thought at first. We'll have to supply the future folks with what they'll need to establish themselves in the past, but that can be done under normal manufacturing processes and at a fraction of the tunnel cost. Someone will have to do some rather rapid planning to calculate how much of our manufacturing processes and resources will have to be converted for a time to the making of wheelbarrows, hoes, axes, plows and other similar items, but that's simply a matter of mathematics. We'll have to face up for the next few years to considerable shortages of meat and dairy products and other agricultural items, I suppose, because we'll have to send breeding stock to the Miocene, but all of this we can do. It may pinch us a bit, but it can be done. The tunnels were the big job and Chapman's consortium will do the job there, if we let them."

"How about all those banner-carrying kids who say they want to go back in time?" asked Cunningham. "I say let them go. It would clear the streets of them and for a long time a lot of people have been yelling about population pressure. We may have the answer here."

"You're being facetious, of course," said the President, "but. . . ."

"I can assure you, sir, I'm not in the least facetious. I mean it."

"And I agree with you," said the President. "My reasons may not be yours, but I do think we should not try to stop anyone who wants to go. Not, perhaps, back to the era where the future people plan to go. Maybe to an era a million years later than the future people. But before we allow them to go they must have the same ecological sense and convictions the future people have. We can't send people back who'll use up the resources we already have used. That would make a paradox I don't pretend to understand, but I imagine it might be fatal to our civilization."

"Who would teach them this ecological sense and conviction?"

"The people from the future. They don't all need to go back into the past immediately. The most of them, of course, but some can stay here until later. In fact, they have offered to leave a group of specialists with us who will teach as much of what has been—no, I guess that should be 'will be'—learned in the next five hundred years. For one, I think this offer should be accepted.''

"So do I,'' said Williams. "Some of what they teach us may upset a few economic and social applecarts, but in the long run we should be far ahead. In twenty years or less we could jump five hundred years ahead, without making the mistakes that our descendants on the old world line made.''

"I don't know about that,'' said Douglas. "There's too many factors in a thing like that. I'd have to think about it for a while.''

"There's just one thing that we are forgetting,'' Sandburg said. "We can go ahead and plan, of course. And we have to do it fast. We have to be well along to a working, operating solution to the crisis that we face in a month or so or time will begin running out. But the point I want to make is this—the solution, the planning may do us little good if we aren't able to wipe out, or at least control, the monsters.''

45

THE kids out in the street might be the ones, Wilson told himself, with the right idea. There was some well-founded fascination in starting over once again, with the slate wiped clean and the record clear. Only trouble was, he thought, that even starting over, the human race might still repeat many of its past mistakes. Although, going back, it would take some time to make them and there'd be the opportunity, if the will were there, to correct them before they got too big, too entrenched and awkward.

Alice Gale had talked about a wilderness where the White House once had stood and Dr. Osborne, on the ride from Fort Myer to the White House, had expressed his doubt that the trend which had made the White House park a wilderness could be stopped—it had gone too far, he said. You are too top-heavy, he had said; you are off your balance.

Perhaps the trend had gone too far, Wilson admitted to himself—big government growing bigger; big business growing fatter and more arrogant; taxes steadily rising, never going down; the poor becoming ever poorer and more and more of them despite the best intentions of a welfare-conscious society; the gap between the rich and poor, the government and the public, growing wider by the year. How could it have been done differently, he wondered. Given the kind of world there was, how could circumstances have been better ordered?

He shook his head. He had no idea. There might be men who

could go back and chart the political, economic and social growth and show where the errors had been made, putting their fingers on certain actions in a certain year and saying here is where we made one error. But the men who could do this would be theorists, working on the basis of many theories which in practice would not stand the test.

The phone on his desk rang and he picked it up.

"Mr. Wilson?"

"Yes."

"This is the guard at the southwest gate. There is a gentleman here who says that he must see you on a matter of importance. Mr. Thomas Manning. Mr. Bentley Price is with him. Do you know them, sir?"

"Yes. Please send them in."

"I'll send an escort with them, sir. You'll be in your office?"

"Yes. I'll wait here for them."

Wilson put the receiver back into its cradle. What could bring Manning here, he wondered. Why should he have to come in person? A matter of importance, he had said. And Bentley—for the love of God, why Bentley?

Was it, he wondered, something further about the UN business?

He looked at his watch. The cabinet meeting was taking longer than he'd thought. Maybe it was over and the President had gotten busy with some other matters. Although that would be strange—Kim ordinarily would have squeezed him in.

Manning and Bentley came into the room. The guard stopped at the door. Wilson nodded at him. "It's all right. You can wait outside."

"This is an unexpected pleasure," he said to the two, shaking their hands. "I seldom see you, Tom. And Bentley. I almost never see you."

"I got business elsewhere," Bentley said. "I get my legs run off. I'm running all the time."

"Bentley just got in from West Virginia," Manning said. "That's what this visit is about."

"There was this dog in the road," said Bentley, "and then a tree came up and hit me."

"Bentley took a picture of a monster standing in the road," said Manning, "just as it disappeared."

179

"I got her figured now," said Bentley. "It saw the camera pointed at it and it heard it click. Them monsters don't stay around when they see something pointed at them."

"There was another report or two of one disappearing," Wilson said. "A defense mechanism of some sort, perhaps. It's making it tough for the boys out hunting them."

"I don't think so," said Manning. "Forcing them to disappear may be as good as hunting them."

He unzipped a thin briefcase he was carrying and took out a sheaf of photos. "Look at this," he said.

He slid the top photo across the desk to Wilson.

Wilson took a quick look, then fixed his gaze on Bentley. "What kind of trick photography is this?" he asked.

"There ain't no tricks," said Bentley. "A camera never lies. It always tells the truth. It shows you what is there. That's what really happens when a monster disappears. I was using a fast film. . . ."

"But dinosaurs!" yelled Wilson.

Bentley's hand dipped into his pocket and brought out an object. He handed it to Wilson. "A glass," he said. "Take a look with it. There are herds of them, off in the distance. You can't do tricks of that sort."

The monster was hazed, a sort of shadow monster, but substantial enough that there could be no doubt it was a monster. Back of it, the dinosaurs, three of them, were in sharp focus.

"Duckbills," said Manning. "If you showed that photograph to a paleontologist, I have every expectation he could give you an exact identification."

The trees were strange. They looked like palm trees, others like gigantic ferns.

Wilson unfolded the magnifier, bent his head close above the photo, shifted the glass about. Bentley had been right. There were other strange creatures spread across the landscape, herds of them, singles, pairs. A small mammal of some sort cowered in hiding underneath a shrub.

"We have some blowups," Manning said, "of the background. Want to look at them?"

Wilson shook his head. "No, I'm satisfied."

"We looked it up in a geology book," said Bentley. "That there is a Cretaceous landscape."

"Yes, I know," said Wilson.

He reached for the phone. "Kim," he said, "is Mr. Gale in his room? Thank you. Please ask him to step down."

Manning laid the rest of the photos on the desk. "They are yours," he said. "We'll be putting them on the wire. We wanted you to know first. You thinking the same thing that I am?"

Wilson nodded. "I suppose I am," he said, "but no quotation, please."

"We don't need quotes," said Manning. "The picture tells the story. The monster, the mother monster, I would suppose you'd call it, was exposed to the time travel principle when it came through the tunnel. The principle was imprinted on its mind, its instinct, whatever you may call it. It transmitted knowledge of the principle to the young—a hereditary instinct."

"But it took time tunnels, mechanical contraptions, for the humans to do it," Wilson objected. "It took technology and engineering. . . ."

Manning shrugged. "Hell, Steve, I don't know. I don't pretend to know. But the photo says the monsters are escaping to another time. Maybe they'll all escape to another time, probably to the same time. The escape time bracket may be implanted on their instinct. Maybe the Cretaceous is a better place for them. Maybe they have found this era too tough for them to crack, the odds too great."

"I just thought of something," said Wilson, "the dinosaurs died out. . . ."

"Yeah, I know," said Manning. He zipped the briefcase shut. "We better go," he said. "We have work to do. Thanks for seeing us."

"No, Tom," said Wilson. "The thanks are yours and Bentley's. Thanks for coming over. It might have taken days to get this puzzled out. If we ever did. . . ."

He stood and watched them go, then sat down again.

It was incredible, he thought. Yet it did make a lopsided sort of sense. Humans were too prone to think in human grooves. The monsters would be different. Again and again the people from the future had emphasized they must not be regarded as simple monsters, but rather as highly intelligent beings. And that intelligence, no doubt, would be as alien as their bodies. Their intelligence and ability would not duplicate human intelligence and ability. Hard as it might be to understand, they might be able to do by instinct a thing that a human would require a machine to accomplish.

Maynard Gale and Alice came into the room so quietly that he did not know they were there until he looked up and saw them standing beside the desk.

"You asked for us," said Gale.

"I wanted you to look at these," said Wilson. "The top one first. The others are detail blowups. Tell me what you think."

He waited while they studied the photos. Finally, Gale said, "This is the Cretaceous, Mr. Wilson. How was the photo taken? And what has the monster to do with it?"

"The photographer was taking a picture of the monster. As he took it, at the moment he took it, the monster disappeared."

"The monster disappeared?"

"This is the second report of one disappearing. The second that I know of. There may have been others. I don't know."

"Yes," said Gale, "I suppose that it is possible. They're not like us, you know. The ones that came through the tunnel experienced time travel—an experience that would have lasted for only a fraction of a second. But that may have been enough."

He shuddered. "If that is true, if after such an exposure, they are able to travel independently in time, if their progeny are able to travel independently in time, if they can sense and learn and master such a complex thing so well, so quickly, it's a wonder that we were able to stand up against them for these twenty years. They must have been playing with us, keeping us, protecting us for their sport. A game preserve. That is what we must have been. A game preserve."

"You can't be sure of that," said Wilson.

"No, I suppose not. Dr. Wolfe is the man you should consult about this. He would know. At least, he could make an educated guess."

"But you have no doubt?"

"None," said Gale. "This could be a hoax?"

Wilson shook his head. "Not Tom Manning. We know one another well. We worked on the *Post*, right here, together. We were drinking companions. We were brothers until this damn job came between us. Not that he has no sense of humor. But not in a thing like this. And Bentley. Not Bentley. The camera is his god. He would use it for no unworthy purpose. He lives and breathes his cameras. He bows down before them each night before he goes to bed.''

''So then we have evidence the monsters flee into the past. Even as we fled.''

''I think so,'' said Wilson. ''I wanted your opinion. You know the monsters and we do not.''

''You'll still talk with Wolfe?''

''Yes, we'll do that.''

''There is another matter, Mr. Wilson, that we have wanted to talk with you about. My daughter and I have talked it over and we are agreed.''

''What is that?'' asked Wilson.

''An invitation,'' said Gale. ''We're not sure you will accept. Perhaps you won't. We may even offend you with it. But many other people, I think, would accept the invitation. To many it would have a great attraction. I find it rather awkward to phrase it, but it is this: When we go back into the Miocene, if you wish to do so, you would be welcome to go along with us. With our particular group. We should be glad to have you.''

Wilson did not move. He tried to find words and there were no words.

Alice said, ''You were our first friend, perhaps our only real friend. You arranged the matter of the diamonds. You have done so many things.''

She stepped quickly around the desk, bent to kiss him on the cheek.

''We do not need an answer now,'' said Gale. ''You will want to think about it. If you decide not to go with us, we'll not speak of it again. The invitation, I think, is issued with the knowledge that in all probability, your people will be using the time tunnels to go back into an era some millions of years in the past. Much as it might be hoped, I have the feeling you will not be able to escape the crisis that overtook our ancestors (which are you, of course) on the original time track.''

''I don't know,'' said Wilson. ''I honestly do not know. You will let me think about it.''

"Certainly," said Gale.

Alice bent close, her words a whisper. "I do so hope you'll decide to come with us," she said.

Then they were gone, as silently, as unobtrusively as they had come.

The dusk of evening was creeping into the room. In the press lounge a typewriter clicked hesitantly as the writer sought for words. Against the wall the teletypes muttered querulously. One button on Judy's phone console kept flashing. But not Judy's console anymore, he thought. Judy was gone. The plane that was taking her to Ohio was already heading westward.

Judy, he said to himself. For the love of God, what got into you? Why did you have to do it?

It would be lonely without her, he knew. He had not known until now, he realized, how much she had kept him from loneliness, had been a bulwark against the loneliness a man could feel even when with people he thought of as his friends. She had not needed to be with him, only the thought that she was somewhere nearby was quite enough to banish loneliness, to bring gladness to the heart.

She still would be near, he thought. Ohio was not distant; in this day, nowhere in the world was distant. Phones still worked and letters went by mail, but there was a difference now. He thought of how he might phrase a letter if he wrote her, but he knew he'd never write.

The phone rang. Kim said, "The meeting's over. He can see you now."

"Thank you, Kim," said Wilson. It had slipped his mind that he'd asked to see the President. It seemed so long ago, although it hadn't been. It just had been that so much had happened.

When he came into the office, the President said, "I'm sorry you were kept waiting, Steve. There was so much that had to be talked over. What is it that you have?"

Wilson grinned. "Not quite so grim as when I tried to reach you. I think it's better now. There was a rumor out of the U.N."

"This Russian business?"

"Yes, the Russian business. Tom Manning phoned. His UN man—Max Hale, you know him."

"I don't think I've ever met him. I read him. He is sound."

"Hale heard that the Russians would push for the international dropping of nuclear weapons on the areas where the monsters might be.''

''I had expected something of this sort,'' said the President. ''They'd never be able to pull it off.''

''I think it's academic now, anyhow,'' said Wilson. ''These just came in.'' He laid the photos on the desk. ''Bentley Price took the shot.''

''Price,'' said the President. ''Is he the one. . . .''

''He's the one all the stories are about. Drunk a good part of the time, but a top-notch photographer. The best there is.''

The President studied the top photo, frowning. ''Steve, I'm not sure I understand this.''

''There's a story that goes with it, sir. It goes like this. . . .''

The President listened closely, not interrupting. When Wilson finished, he asked. ''You really think that's the explanation, Steve?''

''I'm inclined to think so, sir. So does Gale. He said we should talk with Wolfe. But there was no question in Gale's mind. All we have to do is keep pushing them. Push enough of them into the past and the rest will go. If there were more of them, if we had as few weapons as the people of five hundred years from now had when they first reached Earth, they probably would try to stay on here. We'd offer plenty of fighting, be worthy antagonists. But I think they may know when they are licked. Going back to the Cretaceous, they'll still have worthy opponents. Formidable ones, Tyrannosaurus rex and all his relatives. The Triceratops. The coelurosaurs. The hunting dinosaurs. Hand-to-hand combat, face-to-face. They might like that better than what humans have to offer. More glory in it for them.''

The President sat thoughtfully silent. Then he said, ''As I recollect, the scientists have never figured out what killed off the dinosaurs. Maybe now we know.''

''That could be,'' said Wilson.

The President reached for the callbox, then pulled back his hand.

''No,'' he said. ''Fyodor Morozov is a decent sort of man. What he did this morning was in the line of duty, on orders that he had to carry out. No use to phone him, to point it out to him. He'll find out when the picture hits the street. So will the people up at the UN. I'd like to see their faces. I'd say it spikes their guns.''

"I would say so, sir,'' said Wilson. "I'll take no more of your time. . . .''

"Stay for a minute, Steve. There's something you should know. A sort of precautionary knowledge. The question may come up and you should know how to field it. No more than half a dozen of our men know this and they won't talk. Neither will the future people. It's top secret, unofficially top secret. There is no record. State doesn't know. Defense doesn't know.''

"I wonder, sir, if I should. . . .''

"I want you to know,'' said the President. "Once you hear it you are bound by the same secrecy as the others. You've heard of the Clinton Chapman proposal?''

"I have heard of it. I don't like it. The question came up this morning and I refused comment. Said it was only rumor and I had no knowledge of it.''

"Neither do I like it,'' said the President. "But so far as I am concerned, he's going to be encouraged to go ahead. He thinks he can buy time travel; he thinks he has it in his hand; he can fairly taste it. I have never seen a more obvious case of naked greed. I'm not too sure his great, good friend Reilly Douglas may not have a touch of that same greed.''

"But if it's greed. . . .''

"It's greed, all right,'' said the President. "But I know something that he doesn't know and if I can manage it, he won't know it until it's too late to do him any good. And that is this: What the future people used was not time travel as we think of it; it is something else. It serves the same purpose, but it's not time travel as traditionally conceived. I don't know if I can explain this too well, but it seems there is another universe, coexistent with ours. The people of the future know it's there, but there is only one thing they really know about it. That is that the direction of time's flow in the second universe is exactly the opposite of ours. Its future flows toward our past. The people of the future traveled into their past by hooking onto the future flow of this other universe . . .''

"But that means. . . ."

"Exactly," said the President. "It means that you can go into the past, but you can't come back. You can travel pastward, but not futureward."

"If Chapman knew this, the deal would be off."

"I suppose it would be. He's not proposing to build the tunnels from patriotic motives. Do you think badly of me, Steve, for my deception—my calculated dishonesty?"

"I'd think badly of you, sir, if there really were a chance for Chapman to do what he means to do and you did not stop him. This way, however, the world gets help and the only ones who are hurt are men who, for once, overreached themselves. No one will feel sorry for them."

"Someday," said the President, "it will be known. Someday my dishonesty will catch up with me."

"When it does," said Wilson, "and sometime, of course, it will, a great guffaw will go around the world. You'll be famous, sir. They'll build statues of you."

The President smiled. "I hope so, Steve. I feel a little sneaky."

"One thing, sir," said Wilson. "Just how tight is this secret of yours?"

"I feel it's solid," said the President. "The people you brought up from Myer told our National Academy people—only three of them. They reported back to me. The future scientists and the men who talked with them. To me alone. By this time, I had gotten wind of Chapman's deal and I asked them to say nothing. Only a few of the future scientists worked on the project that sent the people back; only a handful of them know what actually is involved. And as it happens, they all are here. Something like the diamonds. They all are here because they felt we were the one nation they could trust. The word has been passed along at Myer. The future scientists won't talk. Neither will our men."

Wilson nodded. "It sounds all right. You mentioned the diamonds. What became of them?"

"We have accepted temporary custody. They are locked

away. Later, after all of this is over, we'll see what can be done with them. Probably rather discreet sales of them, with a suitable cover story provided. A few at a time. With the money put in escrow for later distribution to the other nations.''

Wilson rose and moved toward the door. Halfway there, he stopped and turned. ''I'd say, Mr. President, that it's going very well.''

''Yes,'' said the President. ''After a bad start, it is going well. There's still a lot to do, but we are on the way.''

Someone was at Judy's desk when Wilson returned. The room was dark. There were only the flashing lights on the console and they were not being answered.

''Judy?'' asked Wilson hesitantly. ''Judy, is that you?'' Knowing that it couldn't be, for by now she was probably landing in Ohio.

''I came back,'' said Judy. ''I got on the plane and then got off again. I sat at the airport for hours, wondering what to do. You are a son of a bitch, Steve Wilson, and you know you are. I don't know why I got off the plane. Getting off, I don't know why I ca~ ~re.''

He strode across the room and stood beside her.

''But, Judy. . . .''

''You never asked me to stay. You never really asked me.''

''But I did. I asked you.''

''You were noble about it. That's the trouble with you. Noble. You never got down on your knees and begged me. And now my baggage is headed for Ohio and I. . . .''

He reached down and lifted her from the chair, held her close.

''It's been a rough two days,'' he said. ''It's time for the two of us to be going home.''